MOVIE NOVELIZATION

SIMON SPOTLIGHT

An imprint of Simon & Schuster Children's Publishing Division
1230 Avenue of the Americas, New York, New York 10020
The Croods © 2013 DreamWorks Animation L.L.C.
All rights reserved, including the right of reproduction in whole or in part in any form.
SIMON SPOTLIGHT and colophon are registered trademarks of Simon & Schuster, Inc.
For information about special discounts for bulk purchases, please contact Simon & Schuster Special Sales at 1-866-506-1949 or business@simonandschuster.com.
Manufactured in the United States of America 1212 OFF
First Edition 10 9 8 7 6 5 4 3 2 1
ISBN 978-1-4424-3071-6
ISBN 978-1-4424-6154-3 (eBook)

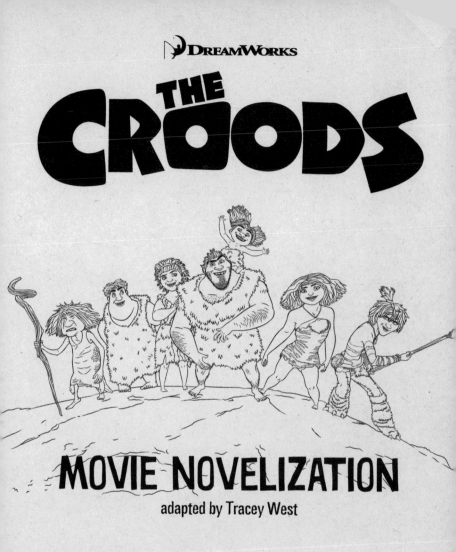

THE CROODS

MOVIE NOVELIZATION

adapted by Tracey West

Simon Spotlight

New York London Toronto Sydney New Delhi

PROLOGUE

With every sun comes a new day. A new beginning. A hope that things will be better today than they were yesterday.

My name's Eep. For a long time there was no hope for me or my family, the Croods. We're cavemen. Most days were spent in our cave, in the dark. Night after night, day after day. Yep. Home sweet home. When we did go out, we struggled to find food in a harsh and hostile world. And I struggled to survive my family.

We were the last ones around. There used to be neighbors. The Gorts were smashed by a mammoth. The Horks got swallowed by a sand snake. The Erfs perished from a mosquito bite. And the Throgs were wiped out by the common cold. And the Croods . . . we made it because of my dad. He was strong, and he followed the rules, the *ones painted on our cave walls:* ANYTHING NEW IS BAD. CURIOSITY IS BAD. GOING OUT AT NIGHT IS BAD. *Basically, anything fun is bad. Welcome to my world.*

But this is a story about how all that changed in an instant. Because what we didn't know was that our world was about to come to an end. And there were no rules on our cave wall to prepare us for that.

CHAPTER I

The morning sun shone on the rocky surface of a red, dusty canyon. A shaft of light illuminated a huge boulder that blocked the entrance to the Croods Cave.

Inside the cave, Grug Crood saw the sliver of light creeping around the edges of the boulder. The long, dark night was finally over. It was time to start the day. And on this day, the Croods would be emerging from the safety of their cave to find food.

A muscled mountain of a man wearing the fur from some massive animal, Grug pushed the boulder aside with a grunt. Then he rushed outside.

"Raaar! Grooooowwwllll! ERF! ERF! Glaaablllth!"

He flailed his arms like a wild beast, picking up clumps of dirt and throwing them. Then he grabbed a huge rock and hurled it.

Panting, Grug stopped and scanned the area around the cave. He had the finest threat display of any caveman. It was guaranteed to scare away anything dangerous that might be lurking outside the cave, waiting for the Croods to emerge. It looked like the coast was clear, so Grug took a deep breath and prepared to bellow the signal that it was safe to come out.

But before he could signal, his teenage daughter Eep pounced out of the cave, growling and pawing the air like some ferocious cat.

"Grrrrrrrr!" she growled.

"You're supposed to wait for my signal, Eep," Grug scolded.

From the corners of her eyes, Eep spotted a pack of furry Liyotes slinking toward them, sniffing with their canine noses. She could see the hunger in their round eyes, and she knew that their reptilian legs and tails gave them extraordinary agility.

"Aaaaargh!" Eep leaped toward them, frightening them, and the Liyotes quickly scattered. A few of them pounced on Grug, and he quickly swatted away the dog-size creatures.

Eep climbed up onto a rock shelf overhanging the cave and leaned back, soaking up the sun. She wore a dress of striped fur that complemented her thick mass of red hair. Her green eyes shone with happiness as she felt the warm rays on her skin.

"We've been in that cave forever," she said, grateful to finally be free.

"Three days is not forever," her father countered.

"It is with this family," Eep shot back.

Grug put his huge hands on his hips. "Eep, will you come down here? You're being so dramatic."

"Ruff! Ruff! Ruff!"

Eep's little sister, Sandy, bounded out of the cave on all fours, barking and snorting in her threat display. She raced off into the canyon.

"No, no, no, Sandy, come back," Grug scolded. "Remember the signal. Good girls wait for the signal."

Grug's wife, Ugga, shot out of the cave after Sandy. She grunted a few times and waved her hands around, but her heart wasn't in her threat display. She was too focused on catching her daughter.

Grug sighed. Wasn't anyone following the rules today? "Ugga!"

"As soon as I get Sandy, I'll go back in, and you can give the signal," she promised.

"But you're already out now," Grug said, shaking his head.

"I am waiting for the signal, Dad!" came a cheerful

voice from inside the cave. It was Thunk, Eep's nine-year-old brother.

"Never mind, Thunk," Grug said, his voice defeated. "Just come out."

But Thunk liked obeying rules as much as his dad liked making them. "Uhh, but if you don't give me the signal, how do I know you're my dad?" Thunk asked.

"The signal isn't so you know it's me," Grug explained. "It's so you know I wasn't eaten by an animal."

Thunk was silent for a moment while he processed this.

"Then why is the signal an animal noise?" he asked. "I mean, doesn't that just confuse things?"

Grug sighed again.

"I'm still waiting for the signal," Thunk said.

Grug knew there was no way to win the argument. He took a deep breath.

"Hoo-hoo! Hoo-hoo!"

Thunk charged out of the cave, growling. He was half as tall as his dad, but just as wide, and they both shared the same broad face and bushy brown hair. Thunk ran right into Grug, nearly knocking him over. Then he picked up a big boulder, mimicking his dad's threat display. He threw it, and it hit the cliff wall, then bounced off and knocked Grug down for real this time.

None of the Croods were alarmed by this. Grug had been plowed down by things bigger than that boulder, and he always got back on his feet.

Ugga scooped up Sandy and headed back toward the cave.

"Mom, we're ready to leave!" she called. She waited, but there was no answer. "Mom!"

A tiny, white-haired woman scurried out of the cave.

"Still alive!" Gran reported, revealing one shiny white tooth as she grinned.

Grug looked disappointed. "It's still early," he mumbled.

"And you're still fat," Gran shot back cheerfully.

Grug shrugged off the insult. "Breakfast formation!" he announced in a booming voice.

The family swiftly fell into place, stepping into V formation with Grug at the lead.

"I want to see some real caveman action out there!" Grug barked, like a commander addressing his troops. "We do this fast. We do this loud, we do this as a family, and never not be afraid. Go!"

"Yay, breakfast!" Thunk cheered, as the Croods ran out of the canyon and into the open desert, where they might finally be able to scrounge up some food.

They ran . . . and ran . . . and ran . . . until they finally came to a stop miles later, exhausted.

"Yay . . . breakfast . . . ," Thunk said again between pants.

Once they arrived at their hunting grounds, the Croods spotted food right away. A huge Ramu nest built in a stand of rocks contained one large, blue egg.

Grug motioned for the family to take shelter behind a nearby rock. Stealing an egg from a nest was a tricky business. If the mother bird was nearby, she would do everything she could to protect it.

He turned to the others. "Okay, who's up?"

Eep's hand shot into the air. She loved hunting.

Thunk didn't really like taking chances, but he raised his hand anyway. He didn't want to disappoint his dad.

"You guys can flip for it," Grug said. He picked up Gran and tossed her. "Call her in the air."

"Heads!" Eep cried out.

Gran landed headfirst in the sand, her skinny legs wiggling wildly and the tail on her lizard-skin dress pointing up to the sky.

"Tails. Thunk's in," Grug announced. "Positions!"

The family moved back and away from one another, forming a wide line between the desert and the canyon, like a sports team ready for the next play.

"Okay, Thunk," Grug said. "Go!"

Thunk broke from the line and dashed toward the nest. He grabbed the egg and raced back toward his family.

"Way to go! Take it to the cave!" Grug cheered.

Thunk ran past Grug, starting on the long journey back to Crood Canyon. Then a loud shriek sent a chill of fear through him.

"Cawwwwwww!" A large Ramu bird ran up behind Thunk, surprisingly swift on her thick legs. She thudded into him with her curved horns, and Thunk lost his grip on the egg. The bird caught the egg in her beak.

"Release the baby," Grug ordered.

Eep raced toward the bird, holding out Sandy in front of her. The little girl's pigtails bobbed up and down as they sped across the desert. When they closed in on the Ramu, Sandy chomped down on the bird's feet with her two big front teeth. With the bird distracted, Ugga jumped onto her back and climbed up to her head, pulling the egg from her beak.

But before the Croods could celebrate victory, some Trip Gerbils intervened. The small, furry creatures looked cute, but they were extremely hazardous. Each pair of gerbils was connected by a long tail, and they used it to trip their victims. The Trip Gerbils were just as hungry as any other creature in the desert, and the egg looked like a tasty meal.

While Ugga steadied herself so she could toss the egg to Grug, the Trip Gerbils sprang into action. They wrapped their tail around the bird's legs, and the bird fell down hard, beak-first. Ugga tumbled off the bird, and the egg fell out of her hands. The Trip Gerbils quickly recovered it and ran off.

"Mom! Intercept!" Ugga cried.

Gran reached out with her cane, hooked the gerbils by the middle of their tail, and whipped them over her shoulder. The egg dropped down and she caught it, then began to dribble it toward the canyon.

A sneaky group of Liyotes jumped out from behind the rocks, swarming Gran. They knocked her down, stole the egg, and zipped across the desert as fast as lightning.

"Old lady down!" Gran yelled. "Eep, avenge me!"

Hidden behind a small bush, Eep waited until the Liyotes passed—and then she pounced. Targeting the Liyote with the egg, she jumped on him and tackled him. The egg was hers!

"Thanks!" she said, leaping away.

But a bunch of Jackrobats quickly circled her. Fast and furry, each Jackrobat had a fluffy white tail; pointy ears; a wide, flat nose; and sharp fangs. They tripped her up, and Eep tossed the egg to Grug.

"Dad! Heads up!" she called out.

Grug caught the egg and ran past the entrance of a small cave, accidentally stepping on the tail of a sleeping Bear Owl. He stood up, tall as Grug, golden eyes flashing, and then chased after Grug, his long, sharp claws kicking up dirt as he ran.

Grug dodged the Bear Owl, passing the egg to Thunk. Thunk caught it just as a huge, spotted Girelephant bore down on him from behind, lifting him up with his large tusks. The Bear Owl caught up to the Girelephant, causing the larger animal to charge forward in fear. Now the Liyotes joined the chase, following by a flock of angry Ramu birds.

The Girelephant caught up to the rest of the Croods, and Grug tossed them one by one onto the back of the great beast. It was a drastic move, but the only way to outrun the swarm of creatures chasing them.

"Dad, can we eat now?" Thunk asked.

"Just wait till we get home," Grug replied. "Eep, put on the brakes."

The Croods hung on as tightly as they could. Eep tumbled from the beast's head and caught one of the tusks, saving herself just in time. Then she slammed her heels on the ground and dug into the dirt, causing the Girelephant to slow down, but the angry Bear Owl was still on the chase and getting closer. They had to get back to the safety of Crood Canyon. Now.

Grug jumped to the other tusk and pulled down. The beast crashed into the rocky entrance of the canyon, and the Croods were thrown in. When the dust cleared, Grug emerged, holding up the egg. Victory!

"Who's hungry?" he asked.

"All right!" cheered Thunk. "Good one, Dad."

Grug smiled. "Here you go, Thunk. Drink up." He tossed the egg to his son . . . who couldn't get ahold of it. It dropped and cracked open.

"Sorry, Dad," Thunk said glumly.

Ugga quickly scooped it up. "Looks like fast food tonight!"

She gave a taste of the leaky egg to Sandy and then took a sip herself. The egg went to Gran, then to Eep, and then to Thunk. He passed it over to Grug—but by now the egg was empty.

"That's all right. I ate last week," Grug said, trying to sound like it was no big deal. His family had been fed, and that was the most important thing.

A shadow reached his feet, and he looked up to see the sun beginning to set behind the canyon wall. It would be dark soon. It was time to head back into the cave.

CHAPTER 2

The Croods reached the entrance of their cave just as the last rays of sun streaked the twilight sky with shades of purple and blue.

"Come on, come on!" Grug urged. "Darkness brings death! We know this!"

Ugga went inside first and picked up a heavy branch.

"The moon is full. Bath night," she announced.

Gran made a face and tried to sneak away.

"You too, Mom," Ugga said firmly.

"Run for your life!" Gran cried, but Ugga grabbed her and pulled her back before she could take another step.

"I don't want to lose my protective layer," Gran complained.

Ugga sighed. "Mom, you've got ants." She picked up Sandy, and the little girl gripped a stalactite hanging down from the top of the cave.

Whack! Ugga gave Sandy a smack with the stick, and dirt and bugs flew off her. Sandy giggled happily.

"See? Sandy doesn't fuss," Ugga said. She clapped her hands, and Sandy let go, hitting the hard cave floor and then going on her way. Gran still wasn't having any of it.

Grug stepped into the cave and looked around. "Is Eep still out there?" he asked.

"You know she hates the cave, Grug," Ugga reminded him.

Outside, Eep had climbed up the face of the cave. Even though the moon was already visible in the twilight sky, it wasn't quite dark yet, and Eep wasn't about to miss the last little bit of sun. She climbed higher, scaling the sheer face of the rock wall like some kind of lizard. She addressed the dwindling rays of sunlight. "Please come back tomorrow."

Back in the cave, Grug grudgingly lifted his arms so Ugga could clean him with the branch. He couldn't understand his oldest child these days.

"How can she not like the cave? It's so cozy," he wondered out loud.

"It is a little dark, Grug," Ugga pointed out.

"It's not that dark," Grug protested.

At that moment, Gran bumped into him. "Out of my way, Thunk!" she growled.

14

"Okay, fine," Grug admitted. "But it's a good cave. It's kept Croods alive for generations."

"It's a good cave, honey," Ugga assured him. "A great cave."

Grug looked into her warm brown eyes, grateful. "Thank you."

As Ugga batted the bugs off him, Grug looked around the cave, the only home he had ever known. In the fading light, he could make out all the paintings that had been drawn by generations of Croods. There was a caveman falling into a sand pit. A caveman being stomped by an angry Girelephant. A caveman being devoured by a huge beast with fangs.

The paintings were warnings, and Grug had always taken them seriously. He had tried to pass the same healthy respect for fear to his children. Thunk and Sandy seemed to understand, and Eep used to, but not anymore. Now Eep was different.

Sandy began to run circles around Grug, laughing. He smiled.

"There's my girl! There's my girl!" he said, egging her on.

Chomp! Sandy jumped up, bit Grug's forearm, and didn't let go.

"Look at those teeth!" Grug said, beaming with

pride. "When she grows into those, she'll be bigger than Eep!"

Then he remembered—Eep was still outside! He had let his mind wander for just a few seconds, and now his daughter was in danger. He rushed outside the cave.

He looked up at Eep's ledge, but she wasn't there.

"Eep! Come on, I gotta close the cave," he grumbled. His eyes wandered up, past the ledge . . . and up some more, where he spotted Eep at the very top of the canyon wall.

"Eep!" he yelled.

Eep looked down, and the realization of how high she'd climbed suddenly hit her. She felt so free and alive!

"Okay! Okay!" she said reluctantly. Couldn't she just stay a few minutes more? Her dad was such a worrier.

"Come on, come on!" Grug urged.

Eep hesitated—and then she saw the Bear Owl charging through the canyon, coming right for her father. Grug instinctively felt the danger and spun around at the same moment.

"EEP! COME DOWN!" he bellowed.

Eep scurried down the rock face as quickly as she could. Grug grabbed a nearby rock and hit the Bear Owl, stunning him. Eep jumped down and darted into the cave, and Grug went right behind her, pushing in place the boulder that blocked the entrance. The Bear Owl recovered and charged again just as Grug slid the barrier into place. He sighed with relief.

The Bear Owl squeezed his paw through the narrow opening of the boulder, reaching around for the Croods. If Grug had closed off the cave one second later, the Bear Owl would have eaten one—or more—of them for dinner.

"That was too close!" Grug fumed.

"I was watching," Eep said coolly. "It was fine."

"What were you doing up there, Eep?" Grug asked.

"I don't know," she answered, shrugging.

Grug tried again. "What were you looking for?"

"Nothing," she replied flatly.

"Well then, why did you go up there?" her father asked, his voice rising in impatience.

"I don't know," Eep shot back, annoyed. Her dad was so frustrating! It was hard dealing with all these strange feelings she was having. How was she supposed to put them into words?

Grug would not give up. "Why don't you know? Stop looking for things. Fear keeps us alive, Eep. Never not be afraid."

Ignoring him, Eep climbed up onto a ledge sticking

out of the cave wall. A tiny crack in the rock let in a sliver of light from outside, and she focused on it.

"What's the point of all this?" she mumbled.

"What was that?" Grug asked.

"I mean, why are we here?" Eep spoke louder, but she still didn't look down at her parents. "What are we doing this for?"

The rest of her family groaned. They had heard this question from Eep before.

"No one said survival was fun," Grug pointed out.

"*Nothing* is fun," Eep complained.

"Hmm? Would you come down here? Eep?" Grug asked impatiently.

Eep didn't answer; she just kept staring at the sliver of light, which was almost gone. Grug started to climb up to the ledge, but Ugga pulled him back down.

"Grug. Off," she said firmly.

"Yes," Grug said. Then he ignored her and started climbing again.

"Off!" Ugga yelled.

Grug climbed back down, pouting. "I just don't see why she needs her own ledge. That's all. That's what this is about."

"She's working through some things and needs some space," Ugga explained gently. She had been a teenage cavegirl once too, so she understood some of what Eep was feeling.

But Grug was a little more hard-headed. "What things? How long is this going to take? Really? She already doesn't listen to me."

At that moment a pebble hit Grug on the head, and he looked up. It had come from Eep's ledge.

"Hey!" Grug protested.

"See? She's listening," Ugga said.

"If she wants to survive, she has to follow our rules," Grug said stubbornly.

Ugga tried to change the subject. "How about a story? Eep loves those."

Grug's mood immediately lightened. "That's a good idea. How about a story?"

Thunk looked excited. "Oh yeah, tell us a story."

"I can't wait to see how this one ends," Gran said sarcastically. She'd heard plenty of Grug's stories before, and they always ended the same way. But she still joined Ugga and Thunk, forming a semicircle on the cave floor. It wasn't like there was anything better to do.

Grug plucked Sandy and Krispy Bear out of a crib made of bones. Krispy Bear was more than just a stuffed toy—he was a lesson. With a look of terror on his face and blacked-out eyes, the poor stuffed bear looked like he had been in the wrong place at the wrong time. He was a warning to the Croods' children to stay safe and follow the rules.

"Can I borrow that?" Grug asked Sandy, and she let him take Krispy Bear from her hands. "Thank you."

Grug called up to the ledge, "Eep! Your old favorite!"

"I haven't played with that thing in years," Eep called back.

Grug ignored her and sat down next to the rest of the family. He held Krispy Bear in front of him.

"Tonight we'll hear the story of Krispy Bear," he began. He paused, waiting for Eep to join them, but she didn't climb down. Grug continued the story.

"A long time ago, this little bear was alive. She was alive because she listened to her father and lived her life in routine and darkness and terror. So she was happy. But Krispy had one terrible problem. She was filled with . . . curiosity!"

"Grug!" Ugga scolded, covering Sandy's ears. "Curiosity" was a bad word in the Croods' household.

"Yes," Grug said with a nod. "And one day, while she was in a tree, the curious little bear wanted to climb to the top."

"What?" Thunk couldn't believe it. Who would do a thing like that?

"And no sooner had she climbed to the top than she saw something new and died," Grug concluded.

Thunk was wide-eyed. "Just like that?"

"Yes!" Grug said. "Her last moments of terror still frozen on her face."

He held out Krispy Bear, and the family recoiled in fear.

"Oh, same ending as every day," Gran said. "Nice."

Poor Thunk was freaked out. "I get it, Dad. I get it. I will never do anything new or different."

Grug thumped him on the back approvingly. "Good man, Thunk."

Ugga yawned. "All right, everyone sharpen your teeth and let's pile up."

The Croods snuggled together in a big heap in the middle of the cave. Grug looked up at Eep's ledge, but his daughter still had her back to them. He sighed and closed his eyes. Maybe he could talk some sense into her in the morning.

Soon the sound of peacefully snoring Croods filled the cave. Only Eep remained awake, restless. Outside, she could hear the snarls and growls of creatures fighting in the darkness, just like she did every night.

And then everything went silent. Curious, Eep sat up. The silence was followed by a strange, musical sound.

Eep quietly crawled down from the ledge and tip-toed around her sleeping family. The sound was fading as she made her way to the cave entrance.

Suddenly a bright light blazed through the gaps around the entrance, a light as bright as the noontime sun. Eep's green eyes grew wide.

What kind of light burned this brightly at night? She had to find out.

CHAPTER 3

The only thing burning brighter than the light outside was the curiosity inside Eep. She pressed her face up against the edge of the boulder, trying to see something. But all she could make out was the light, which was disappearing quickly.

Desperate to see more, she braced her back against the boulder and pushed with all her strength. She might not have inherited her father's love of rules, but she did get his strength. She slowly moved the huge rock aside just enough so she could squeeze through.

At first all she could do was stand still, taking in the wonder of the world around her. She had never been outside at night before—ever. Her heart raced as the hot night wind blew through the canyon, causing her hair to move like a wave. Being outside right now was extremely dangerous and strictly forbidden—and she'd never felt so alive in her life.

Then she noticed that the light was disappearing in the distance, and she snapped back into focus. She *had* to know what was making that light—she just had to. But if every story her dad had ever told her was right, she wouldn't last more than a minute out there.

Her desire to know won out over her fear. She pushed off from the boulder and ran into the canyon, following the light. Her bare feet moved swiftly and quietly across the sandstone, and soon the light was brighter and nearer. She was catching up! Everything was going so well!

Snap! She stepped on a stick, breaking it. She froze, her heart pounding. If anything was nearby looking for a meal, she had just signaled to it.

She looked around. She had reached a rock wall, and now the shadow of a tusked creature loomed there—it looked like some kind of humongous warthog. Thinking quickly, she reached down, grabbed a rock, and threw it at the shadow, hoping to distract it. Then she scaled up the stone wall with amazing speed.

Jumping over the wall, she found herself in a clearing marked by a stone archway. A flaming torch was stuck in the ground, but Eep didn't know it was a torch. She had never seen fire before.

The dancing orange flames made the torch look like a living creature to Eep. She assumed it had run across the canyon—but how? It didn't seem to have any legs. She'd need to get a better look.

Crouching down, she cautiously approached the torch. She didn't notice that the creature with tusks was behind her, watching her. Eep reached out to touch the flame, and the warthog moved in behind her.

Then the wind changed, pushing the flames away from her. It also brought a scent to her nose—an animal scent. She quickly spun around and grabbed the warthog, flipping it over her shoulder. The animal hit the torch and knocked it to the ground.

With her next move, Eep jumped back and grabbed a small boulder. She would make this quick and painless, and the family would eat well for days. Maybe even well enough for her father to forgive her for breaking the rules.

"Nuh! Nuh!" the warthog cried. And then it raised its hands defensively to cover its face.

"No!" it yelled, in what was clearly a human voice.

Stunned, Eep paused. Human hands? A human voice? How could that be? The creature was hideous, with a fur-covered body and a snarling, piglike face.

Slowly the warthog put its hands to the sides of its head and lifted what Eep now realized was a mask on its face. Underneath the ugly animal mask was a handsome boy!

"Aahh!" Eep leaped back in surprise, accidentally dropping the huge rock. It landed on the boy's foot.

"AAHHH!" the boy cried.

Eep knew that a loud noise like that would bring predators from miles away—and her father, too, for that matter. She pounced on the boy, twisting his head sideways. She was still confused about this creature. He had one false head—could he have two?

The boy reached for a stick and whacked Eep on the side of the head.

"Ow!" she cried, letting go of him.

The boy gasped. "Air . . ."

Eep was more puzzled than ever. "You talk."

"I'm a person, like you," the boy said.

Eep lifted the heavy rock that was on top of his foot and picked up the boy with her other hand.

"Sort of . . . like you," he corrected. He had never met anyone so strong!

Eep still didn't know what to make of the stranger. She pried open his mouth and looked around inside. It sure looked like he had a real head. But she couldn't be sure. She sniffed him. He didn't have the deep-down stink of the Croods, but he still smelled human.

Finally she turned him upside down and studied his strange clothing. Leather bands were wrapped around his lower arms. Instead of wearing a big, fur tunic like her father and brother, material covered both of his legs, and furry things covered his feet.

"Okay, could you not . . ." The boy started to giggle. "Hee-hee! That tickles!"

Eep noticed another furry thing around the boy's waist. She had never seen clothing like this before. Curious, she leaned closer.

Two round blue eyes opened up on the furry thing, and Eep let go of the boy, startled.

"Ow!" he cried.

"Quiet!" Eep hissed, placing her foot over the boy's mouth. "I'm not supposed to be out here."

The boy bit her foot, and now it was Eep's turn to yell.

"Ow!"

Back at the cave, Grug's eyes shot open. Something wasn't right. He pushed his family off him and checked on Eep, but she was gone! Grug had never been so scared in his life. Where could she be? What had taken her out of the cave in the middle of the night?

"Eep's gone," Grug told Ugga.

Ugga was suddenly wide awake. "What? Grug!"

"Stay in the cave!" Grug instructed, and with that he went off into the night to find his daughter.

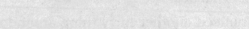

Back outside, Eep and the boy continued to fight. She kicked him in the stomach, and he rolled sideways. The harder the boy tried to defend himself, the harder Eep went after him. Soon he was on his knees, panting.

"Wow, you're really strong," he said.

Then he noticed that the flame on the torch was dwindling, so he moved toward it. Eep blocked his way.

"No! It's mine! I caught it!" she said.

"But it's dying," the boy said. "I can fix it."

Eep didn't budge.

"Please," the boy said, his eyes suddenly filled with fear. "I hate the dark."

Eep understood. She stepped away, and the boy picked up the torch and blew on it. As the light grew brighter, Eep moved into the circle of brightness. She saw the relief on the boy's face as the flame came back to life, and at that moment she felt like they were connected somehow. And even more amazing, this boy seemed to have a magical power over the light!

"It does what you tell it?" Eep asked.

"Well, yeah, sort of," he replied.

"The sun?" she asked next. Only the sun could burn so brightly. Maybe this boy had stolen a piece of it.

But he shook his head. "No, no. Fire."

Eep smiled and waved at the flame. "Hi, Fire."

The boy chuckled. "It's not alive."

Eep was confused. "But you said it was dying."

"Uh, sorry," the boy said with a shrug.

"It comes from where you came from?" Eep asked.

The stranger shook his head. "No, I make it."

Eep grabbed him by the hair. "Make some for me."

"Ow! Okay! It doesn't come out of me," he told her.

But Eep was impatient. "Make. Make. Make it!" She squeezed the boy tightly, but no fire came out. Frustrated, Eep squeezed him harder. Then she heard a popping sound.

Eep quickly dropped the boy, who fell to the ground in a crumpled heap. "Are you dead?" she asked. "Can I have your fire if you're dead?"

The animal around the boy's waist slid off and

picked up two flat rocks. He rubbed them together and placed them on the boy's chest. Sparks flew from the rocks, and the boy sat upright.

"Hey, those are cold!" he complained.

Eep watched the stranger and the animal with awe. The creature was a sloth, but she had never seen one before. His body was covered with reddish fur, and his arms were long and curved, even longer than his legs. His claws were close together and sharp. His face was cute, though, with a little round nose and those big, blue eyes.

"Squirf!" the creature cried, doing a strange little dance on the ground. The boy seemed to understand him.

"You think?" he asked. Then he took two shells from the pouch around his waist. "Listening shells, activate."

He placed one shell on the ground and put his ear to it, listening. The animal did the same.

"I concur," the boy told the creature. He stood up and nodded to Eep. "Tiger girl, we need to leave immediately."

The animal produced a small, round disk with some kind of needle attached to it. The needle spun around, and then stopped. The creature pointed in that direction.

30

Anxious and in a hurry, the boy grabbed Eep by the arm, but she wouldn't move.

"I don't even know you," she pointed out.

The boy sighed impatiently. "I'm Guy."

"Guy?" Eep asked. That didn't sound like any caveman name she had ever heard.

"And this here is Belt," Guy said, pointing to the creature, who was once again wrapped around Guy's waist. "Cook, conversationalist, navigator, also keeps my pants up."

"What are 'pants up'?" Eep asked.

But Guy didn't have time to explain. "Who are you?" he asked.

"Eep," she answered, and Guy held up his hand before she could say anything else.

"Let me clarify, Eep," he said. "The world is ending."

"What?" Eep asked.

"I'm calling it . . ." He opened his arms wide and dramatically wiggled his hands. "The End."

"Da da daaaa!" Belt added, wiggling his long arms along with Guy.

Eep's bushy eyebrows furrowed. "How do you know?"

"I've seen it," Guy replied, and his expression grew dark. "It's coming this way. First, the earth is going to shake. Then it breaks open. Everything falls in. Fire. Lava. I don't mean to sound too dramatic, but aaaaaahhh!"

He waved his arms wildly now, trying to make his point. Beside him, Belt acted out what Guy was describing. He shook his furry little body. His eyes grew wide with terror. And then he flopped on the ground like a fish.

"Believe me," Guy went on, "everything we're standing on, all this right here, will be gone. We've got to get to high ground. I know a mountain, that way—"

Guy pointed to a spot in the distance, to a place no Crood had ever visited.

"It's our only chance," he said, and his voice was serious. He held out a hand. "Come with me."

Eep was torn. Every part of her wanted to follow this boy who could create light in the darkness. She wanted to go to that faraway place, to see something new and different.

But she couldn't leave her family behind.

"I can't," she said.

Guy handed her one of the shells. She looked down at its curved shape—almost like a horn, but prettier and lighter.

Then Guy put the mask back down over his face.

"Okay, here. If you survive, call me."

Eep put her lips on the shell and blew, testing it out. It made a musical sound—the same sound she had heard earlier in the cave. She giggled.

"Thank you," she said, looking up. But Guy was nowhere to be seen. "Hello? Hey!"

The light was gone now, and Eep bumped into something big and furry.

"Dad!" Eep cried.

CHAPTER 4

Grug looked angry and worried at the same time. "Are you hurt? What took you?"

"Nothing," Eep admitted. "I left on my own."

Stunned, Grug released his grip. "You . . . what?"

"Dad, let me explain," Eep began, but the sound of a low growl interrupted her. They both recognized the sound of the Bear Owl.

Seconds later, Grug was dangling by one hand under a log that stretched over a crevice and holding Eep with the other hand. The Bear Owl crossed over the log without noticing them.

"You never let me talk," Eep whispered to her dad.

"You're grounded," Grug said firmly.

When all was clear, they cautiously made their way back to the cave. As the sun rose, the rest of the family met up with them in Crood Canyon.

Ugga's face lit up with joy when she saw her daughter. "Eep!"

"Mom!" Eep ran toward her.

Ugga stroked her daughter's hair for a moment and then looked up at her husband. "Grug! What happened?"

"You know what, I am so mad right now that I can't talk to her," Grug said, stomping past his wife.

"Eep?" Ugga asked, looking to her daughter for an explanation.

Eep knew her mother would understand. "You'll never believe it," she replied. "I found something new."

"NEW?" Ugga, Gran, and Thunk all shouted the word, terrified. The whole family immediately formed a defensive circle around Eep, expecting something bad to happen.

"New is a big problem!" Grug cried, and the family squeezed in tighter around Eep.

Eep pushed through the circle. "Wait. Wait!"

"Eep, stay inside the family kill circle," her mother instructed calmly.

"But it wasn't bad!" Eep insisted.

"New is always bad," Grug said.

"No." Eep shook her head. "He was nice."

Grug thought he might explode with rage. "What? Excuse me? *He?*"

"Well, I thought he was a warthog, but then he turned into a boy," Eep explained.

"Strange. Usually it's the reverse," Gran remarked.

Thunk started to taunt his big sister. "Eep's got a boy hog! Eep's got a boy hog!"

Eep whacked him in the back of the head.

"There was a boy," she explained. "Watch, okay? I'm gonna call him."

She pulled out the shell, put it to her lips, and blew. The unfamiliar sound alarmed everyone in her family. They smacked the shell from her hand and smashed it to pieces.

When the dust cleared, Eep stared at the broken shell on the ground.

"What is wrong with you?" she asked.

"It was dangerous," Grug replied flatly.

Eep could feel the anger rising up inside her. "It was beautiful. You want to see dangerous? Here." She picked up a rock and threw it at Thunk.

"Ow! My sniffer!" he wailed, rubbing his nose.

Grug was losing patience. "Okay, Eep, that's it. We're going back to the cave and you're going to stay there until you're older than . . . her!" He pointed at Gran.

"What?" Eep fumed. "You can't keep me inside forever!"

To show her frustration, she picked up a big rock and slammed it into the ground. It shattered into dust. Still angry, she went to reach for another rock when suddenly a strange groan came up from under the ground.

Creeeeaaaak! Sand rained down from the canyon wall above them, and at their feet, a crack formed on the canyon floor.

"He said this would happen," Eep remarked.

Boom! The ground started to shake violently. The Croods might not have believed Eep's story, but they knew danger when they saw it.

"Get to the cave. Go!" Grug bellowed.

Even Eep couldn't argue with that command. The Croods ran frantically through the canyon, dodging falling boulders and trying not to lose their footing on the quaking ground. Finally the cave entrance came into view, a safe beacon in the middle of chaos.

But the rock walls above the entrance were cracking. Luckily, Grug saw them in time.

"Look out! Stop!" he warned, leaping on his family and tackling them to the ground. Rocks and dust rained down on them, but Grug kept his family safe.

When the earth finally settled, Grug slowly stood,

and the Croods crawled out from underneath him.

"Is everyone okay?" Grug asked.

"Yes," Ugga replied, clutching Sandy. Then she turned. "Grug, the cave. It's gone."

Grug turned to see a pile of rubble where the cave used to be.

"No," he said in disbelief.

He frantically searched through the broken rocks, hoping that if he dug deep enough, he'd find the cave. He picked up two rocks with a handprint that had been split in two. Carefully he fit them back together and lowered his head.

Crood Cave—his home, his family's home, and the home of his ancestors—was gone forever.

Eep stepped carefully through the rubble, waving away clouds of dust. A shaft of light filtered through the dusty veil and she moved toward it, as curious as always. When the air cleared, she gasped.

"You really need to see this," she called to her family.

The Croods gathered around her, their faces filled with awe as they looked down into the valley below. Behind the collapsed canyon wall was a world they had never seen, a world filled with trees and plants and colors.

"We should go there!" Eep exclaimed.

"No. No one is going anywhere," Grug said firmly, pulling her back. "What else did that boy say?"

Before she could reply, a creature swooped down from the sky. It was a huge bird with blue feathers; a short, stubby beak; and a shell on its back—a Turtle Dove. The bird flew over their heads and then doubled back, returning to the New World where it had come from.

They stared at the sky in amazement until a menacing growl roused them. The Bear Owl was back! He roared and charged toward the unprotected Croods. Grug grabbed a giant boulder and rolled it in front of everyone, but the massive Bear Owl just swatted it away.

But by that time, the Croods were already running toward the New World as fast as they could. When they reached the edge, they all jumped together. They landed with a thud on a slope covered with plants and flowers, and then tumbled down the hill.

They had no clue what they would find in the New World, but for the moment, it was a safer option than dealing with the Bear Owl.

CHAPTER 5

It was a steep fall, but the Croods were cavemen, and they were tough. Grug sat up first. He turned to look at the cliff high, high above them. Their old home was up there, buried under a pile of rocks. Thankfully, there was no sign of the Bear Owl.

He stood up, and the others slowly did the same. Grug took a deep breath and took a head count.

"One, two, three, four, five . . ." Grug grinned. Had they finally lost Gran?

But his hopes were dashed as the old woman tumbled down the hill next to him.

"Six," Grug said with a sigh.

Gran sat up, wincing in pain. "Where are we?" she asked.

"I don't know," Grug admitted. "Down. In a lower

place. One thing's for sure, we can't go back the way we came."

The rest of the family looked around, dazed and disoriented. Sandy began to sniff the air. Then she scurried off on all fours, growling.

"Sandy? What is it?" Ugga asked, lunging after her.

Grug reached her first. He grabbed her as she leaped in midair toward something in the bushes. As he pulled her back to him, he saw that she had a tiny creature clamped in her mouth—it was the size of a mouse, but with big, floppy ears; a long trunk; and tiny tusks.

Grug knocked the Mousephant out of his youngest child's mouth. The Mousephant ran back to the bush and then emerged with its entire family, and they all scurried away.

Grug knew his family had to move, but he had no idea what lay ahead. What he did know was that he couldn't be too careful . . . and that they needed to find a new cave. "We can't be out in the open like this," he whispered. "We need a cave. Now step where I step."

The Croods slowly moved through the strange Jungle.

"Okay. Stay quiet. Hopefully nothing big knows we're here yet," Grug whispered.

Grug didn't know it, but something very big *was*

watching them. He cautiously led his family around the plants and trees, stopping every few seconds to see what lay ahead.

"Wait," Grug said, holding out his hand. Then, after he was satisfied, "Okay."

They moved ahead a few more steps when Grug stopped them. "Wait," and then, after a moment, "Okay."

It went on like this for a while as the Croods moved through the dense growth.

"So Dad, just to be clear, are we looking for the exact same cave?" Thunk asked, rambling nervously. "If it was me choosing the cave, I would go with a smaller cave."

Grug didn't answer his son. He was too busy trying to navigate this new place. He wasn't sure if he should look ahead, to see what they were getting into, or look down, to see what they were stepping on, or look behind them, to see if something was chasing them. And then there was all the rustling and chattering in the leaves overhead.

Small, furry Bear Pears hung by their striped tails from the tree branches, watching the Croods with their big orange eyes. Grug ignored them—they looked harmless enough, and he was too focused on getting his family to a cave, any cave, as quickly as possible.

Eep brought up the back of the line, and getting to a cave was the last thing on her mind. There was so much to see! So much that was new and wonderful! She eyed the Bear Pears, marveling at how cute they were with their big, round heads and smaller round bodies.

A leaf fluttered down in front of Grug, and he stopped.

"Wait," he instructed.

He looked up to where the leaf had come from to see that the surrounding trees were filled with dozens of monkeys on low branches. They had black fur marked with patches of white and gold; small, curious faces; and fists that seemed way too big for their tiny bodies.

The rest of the Croods noticed the Punch Monkeys too and looked to Grug for guidance.

"Dad?" Thunk asked.

"I'll take care of this," Grug said confidently. He launched into his threat display.

"Waaaaaaaaargh!" he yelled, flailing his arms and pounding his chest in front of the nearest monkey. But the creature just stared at him.

Grug stopped, confused. Why wasn't it working? Then the Punch Monkey broke into a huge smile.

Thud! The Punch Monkey punched Grug in the face with his big fist. Grug reeled back, surprised, and spun around—right into the fist of another monkey!

Thud! That one punched Grug too.

"All right, Dad, go get 'em," Thunk cheered, as his father faced another monkey and got another punch in the face. "Oh, oh, now you got 'em. Now they're really hitting you. Dad, I got it, just stop running into their fists!"

Thud!

"Hah! I'm loving this," Gran said with a grin.

Thud!

"Grug, when you're done, we should get going," Ugga said impatiently.

Thud! The Punch Monkeys were bouncing Grug back and forth among themselves, whooping and hollering. Then they suddenly scattered.

"That's right! You can't get past this!" Grug said, flexing his massively muscled arm. They must have been frightened away by his sheer brawn, he reasoned.

But he was wrong.

ROAR!

The big thing that had been watching the Croods reared up behind them. In his resting position, his blue, orange, and green fur had made him look like another colorful jungle bush. But now that he was standing up on all four legs, they could see how truly terrifying he was. A huge, tigerlike beast with large fangs in his snarling mouth, the Macawnivore looked hungry. Hungry for Croods.

Grug grabbed the nearest rock and hurled it at the beast. The Macawnivore caught the rock in his right paw and then sprang at the terrified family.

"Go! Go! Go! Go!" Grug urged, as he and his family raced away from the hungry cat. They ran past a tree trunk, and then Grug saw a welcome sight—a cave!

"Cave! Go! Go!" Grug ordered. "Come on, hurry up! Let's go!"

The Croods all ran inside the cave—and then the mouth of the cave snapped shut.

"Hey, look! This cave has a tongue!" Thunk cried, bouncing on a huge pink tongue under his feet. "Awesome!"

This was no cave. The Croods had run right into the mouth of a massive gray Land Whale, making its way through the Jungle!

Luckily, the Land Whale wasn't hungry. It stood up and spit the Croods from its blowhole. They flew above the Jungle for a moment and then landed on the ground in a heap in the middle of a grassy field.

Grug took another quick head count. "One . . . two . . . three . . . four . . . five . . . six . . ."

"And seven," Gran added, "if we're counting Chunky the Death Cat."

The Macawnivore appeared behind them, rising out of some tall grass. He grinned, pleased at the prospect of a big meal.

Then the shadow of the setting sun crossed his face, and the creature looked alarmed. Chunky turned around and quickly retreated into the trees.

"Ha! He's scared of the dark!" Gran cackled, and then she frowned. "Wait . . . *we're* scared of the dark!"

The Croods looked at one another, panicked. Except for Eep, none of them had ever been outside at night before, and there was no cave in sight.

Suddenly, thousands of Piranhakeets flew up out of the grass, forming a huge cloud above the Croods. The red birds had thick, curved beaks. The Croods watched in wonder as the clouds of Piranhakeets flew to the Land Whale and settled on its back. Chirps and shrieks filled the air and then seconds later the birds flew away— leaving only the Land Whale's skeleton behind!

Fear filled the Croods as the skeleton crumbled to the ground.

"Kill circle!" Grug commanded, and the Croods quickly fell into formation, each one grabbing a rock— except for Eep.

Eep knew rocks wouldn't protect them from the ravenous birds. And this time, neither could her dad. She only knew one thing that could help them—a piece of the sun.

Eep dodged out of the family circle toward an animal skull lying in the sand.

"Eep! Eep!" Grug called.

She broke off a curved horn from the top of the skull. Then she put the horn to her lips—and blew.

CHAPTER 6

Guy was walking quickly, determined to reach the Mountain before the earth opened up again. He couldn't stop thinking about Eep, though. It was hard leaving her behind. Hers had been the first friendly—well, mostly friendly—face he had seen in a really long time. Sure, she could pack a punch, but once you got to know her there was something, well, special about her. What would happen to her and her family once the world ended?

She's tough, Guy told himself. *She'll be okay.*

And then he heard the sound of the horn as it echoed across the Jungle. His heart jumped in his chest. That had to be Eep!

Guy raced toward the sound, which led him to a grassy clearing. He saw Eep standing alone, holding the horn. The hungry flock of carnivorous Piranhakeets was flying toward her.

Running as fast as he could, he leaped onto a rock formation that protruded into the clearing. Beneath the rock, the rest of the Croods huddled in fear, but he didn't see them.

As his feet touched down on the rock, he struck two stones together, creating a spark. The birds closed in, blocking Guy's view of Eep. His heart pounded. Was she all right?

Then a tiny flame fluttered to life, and Guy quickly lit a pile of grass at his feet. The fire flared brightly, and he lit his torch from the flame. He jumped down from the rock and held Eep. The frightened birds quickly flew away, a swirling red tornado of tiny monsters. Then Guy heard a growl and turned to see Grug standing there. The big caveman snarled.

"Ta-da!" Guy said, hoping to break the tension.

Grug pushed Eep away from the stranger and then launched into his threat display. No boy was going to pick up his daughter.

"Aaargh! Aauugh!"

Ugga, Thunk, Gran, and Sandy joined in, circling around Guy and Eep. They each performed a threat display, groaning, grunting, and growling.

Guy moved in front of Eep to protect her.

"Cavies!" he cried.

Eep was confused. "Cavies?"

"Cavemen!" Guy explained. "Stand back! They're practically animals. See their bony, sloping foreheads?"

"Oh . . . yeah!" Eep replied, trying to sound enthusiastic.

"The huge primitive teeth?" Guy asked.

Eep nodded. "Er . . . yeah . . ."

"The excessive body hair?" he asked. He pointed at Gran. "That one's even got a tail!"

"Uh . . . yeah," Eep said. She didn't want to admit that she knew them . . . very well.

Guy pulled a stone knife from his belt. "Close your eyes. I'm going to have to take their lives."

Eep quickly slapped the knife away. "No, it won't help," she said with a sigh. For the first time in her life, she felt embarrassed. "They're my family."

Now it was Guy's turn to be confused. "What?"

The Croods kept circling Guy and Eep, but now they were more curious than angry. Besides, this boy didn't seem to pose a threat.

"Ah, the sun is in his hands!" Thunk said, staring at the orange flame glowing from the torch. The other Croods couldn't take their eyes off it either.

"No, no, it's fire," Eep told them.

"Where did it come from?" Ugga asked.

Eep smiled proudly. "He made it."

Grug gripped Guy in a bear hug and squeezed him tightly. "Make some for me!"

"It doesn't come out of him," Eep tried to explain, but Grug wasn't convinced.

"Make it! Make it!" he commanded, squeezing harder.

"You know, you're a lot like your daughter," Guy said hoarsely. Grug finally let go, and the boy dropped to the ground in a heap.

Eep scowled at her father. "Great, now he's broken!" she cried, kneeling next to Guy.

The rest of the Croods were more interested in Guy's torch than in the broken stranger.

"Oh, it's a baby sun!" Ugga exclaimed, moving closer to the torch, which had fallen out of Guy's hand onto the ground. Thunk, Gran, and Sandy joined her, inching toward the bright flame. They sat in a circle around the flame, staring at it with wide eyes.

Grug knew trouble when he saw it.

"Whoa! Stay back! We don't know what it wants," he said, running around the circle. One by one he picked up the members of his family and moved each one a safe distance away. Then he spoke to them in a calm, teacherlike voice.

51

"Now we'll all sit here and wait for the sun to come back," he said. "And tomorrow we'll find a new cave and pretend this never happened."

He gazed into the fire and forced a smile. "Isn't this fun, Eep?"

But when Grug looked around, he realized that Eep wasn't in the circle with them. She was still kneeling beside Guy, trying to revive him.

"Eep, don't touch him!" Grug ordered. "Goodness knows where he's been."

His back was turned for only a moment when Sandy crawled toward the fire and attacked the torch, grabbing the wooden end of it with her teeth. She shook her head violently, like a dog with a bone, and red-hot embers flew everywhere.

"Dad, Sandy's hurting fire!" Thunk tattled.

Grug reached down and scooped up Sandy. She kicked and struggled, refusing to give up the torch. "Sandy! No!" he scolded. "Fire is not a plaything."

Like Sandy, Ugga, Thunk, and Gran still thought the fire was some kind of living creature. To them, the embers looked like tiny glowing insects.

"Aw, what a cute little guy," Ugga said, as an ember floated past her. She reached out a hand to touch it.

"Hey, stay back!" Grug warned.

But nobody listened. They were spellbound by the bright embers that danced in the darkness, and they kept reaching out, trying to snatch one up.

"No, no, no, wait!" Grug yelled. He wanted to stop them, but his hands were full with Sandy.

One of the embers landed on the hem of Thunk's furry tunic. "It likes me!" Thunk cried happily, watching as the ember burrowed into the fur. But his expression quickly changed as the burning ember touched his skin.

"Hey! It's biting me!" he wailed, slapping at it.

A shower of sparks shot up from Thunk's tunic, and he ran furiously around the clearing, trying to get away from the angry creature that was tormenting him. Embers flew off him, landing in the grass and sprouting new fires every time they touched down. Grug looked around at the growing fires. What was happening?

"Ow! You're not my friend!" Thunk yelled, trying to shoo away the flame on his tunic. "Stop touching me!"

"Thunk! Try hiding from it in the tall, dry grass!" Grug suggested. That was a good way to hide from any other predator, wasn't it?

Thunk sprinted through the grass, flailing his arms. A ring of fire blazed up around him as the grass ignited.

"Stop, please! I'm only nine!" he pleaded with a nearby flame.

53

Gran let out a cackle. It was fun to see the shiny sun creature teasing her grandson. But her expression changed to a frown when she noticed a flame on the end of her walking stick.

"Shoo! Shoo!" Gran cried, angrily banging the stick on the ground. A new fire shot up every time the stick hit the grass.

Ugga was still enchanted. "Ooh, more fire babies!" she squealed, racing toward the nearest one with open arms. Thinking they must be hungry, she started throwing sticks on the flames to feed them.

Nearby, Guy finally opened his eyes.

"Hi," Eep said.

"So, your dad, he's trying to kill me," Guy said, his voice hoarse.

"Yeah," Eep said with a nod. Then she smiled. "But I won't let him."

They both turned to look at Grug—and saw him frantically chasing Thunk in circles.

"Hold on, son, come back!" he yelled, throwing rocks at his son's flaming backside.

Thunk craned his head to look down at the flames. "I don't like you anymore!" he wailed to the fire.

Grug still struggled to hold on to Sandy as he chased Thunk. The little girl thought they were playing a fun

54

game. She whacked the torch against every tree, bush, and plant that she passed—and each one burst into flame.

Gran was batting her walking stick against anything she could find.

"Get out! Get out!" she yelled at the fire.

Ugga's little fire babies were growing fast. She uprooted a nice, big redwood tree so they could grow some more.

"Eat up, babies!" she cooed.

Guy's jaw dropped. He had never seen anything like it. The Croods were setting everything on fire! They looked crazed.

Then Gran's walking stick hit a new target—a giant ear of corn. The flame from the stick ignited the ear and set off a chain reaction, setting fire to an entire cornfield.

"Die! Die!" Gran yelled gleefully, beating the stick against the corncob again and again.

Poof! The fire on the end of her cane finally went out. Gran pumped a fist in the air.

"I win!" she cheered.

And then . . . *POP!*

The giant corncob burst out of the ground, causing Gran to be thrown back.

Wham! She slammed into Thunk.

Bam! The corn hit Ugga, who flew up on top of it.

Whack! The ear of corn nailed Grug next. He landed next to Ugga while still holding Sandy, who laughed and clapped her hands. This was the best game ever!

"They're not so scary once you get to know them," Eep assured Guy.

The ear of corn continued to speed across the field like a torpedo being piloted by cavemen. *Slam!* It picked up Eep and Guy.

"Who are you people?" Guy asked, craning his head around Grug's massive body.

"Oh, I'm sorry. We're the Crooooods!" Ugga replied, as the corn picked up speed. "And you are?"

"Guy."

"Hi, Guy!" Eep's family all said at once, waving.

Boom! The ear of corn crashed into a tree, sending its passengers sprawling across the ground. The ear of corn kept going, straight up into the sky, where it joined other ears of corn, all bursting into colorful fireworks. Then popcorn began raining down on the group.

"Wow! Looks like magic!" Thunk said, his eyes filled with wonder. Then one of the giant popcorn pieces fell into his hands, and he sniffed it. "And smells like food."

Popcorn kernels began to bury them.

"Don't eat it," Grug warned. "It's new!"

CHAPTER 7

The popcorn might have been new and forbidden, but the Croods had three good reasons to eat it. One: They were buried in a giant mountain of it and had to get out. Two: They were hungry. And three: It was delicious!

The Croods munched and munched on the popcorn, working their way to the top of the pile. They reached the surface at the same time, bursting through the kernels into the bright morning sunshine.

"Still alive!" they cheered.

Guy had a different strategy. He tunneled his way through the bottom of the pile.

"Come on, keep eating," he urged Belt, who was doing his part to help out. Eep was nice enough, but Guy knew he'd never make it to safety with this crazy clan of cavies tagging along. He'd be safer running through a field of quicksand with a tribe of tigers on his tail. If he wanted to survive, he'd have to escape them.

Finally he reached the end of the pile and burrowed out into the clearing. He looked around to see if he'd been spotted. Eep and her family were close, but they hadn't seen him yet.

Slowly and carefully he tiptoed away from the pile, hoping he wouldn't be noticed. Then he heard Eep's voice and began to make a run for it.

"Hey, where's Guy?" she asked.

She turned and saw Guy sneaking away. In a flash she was on him, pouncing on him like a lion.

"No!" Guy yelled.

Eep lifted him up and looked right into his eyes. "Going somewhere?"

"The Mountain. High ground. End of the world, remember?" he answered impatiently.

"That already happened," Eep said. "It destroyed our cave."

Guy struggled to escape her grip, but she was holding on to him so tightly that he didn't have a chance.

"That was just the *beginning* of the end," he tried to explain. "The *end* of the end is still coming."

Grug frowned at his daughter. "Eep. Drop it."

Eep set Guy down, and he immediately tried to bolt

58

again. But she still had a firm grip on his hand, and he was yanked sharply backward. He sighed.

"We can't let him go!" Eep argued. "What if we don't find a cave before sunset? What if it takes a few days? What if the birds come back?"

Grug thought about this for a moment.

"We need his fire, dummy!" Gran told Grug.

That made sense to Grug. With one swift motion he pulled Guy away from Eep and stuffed him inside a hollow log. Guy's feet stuck out one end, and his head stuck out the other. Belt wriggled his way out of the log, but there wasn't much he could do to help Guy.

"Fine," Grug said to Eep. Then he looked at Guy. "You're staying with us until we find a cave."

"What? No, I'm not!" Guy protested. "Don't make me part of this. Stay here if you want, but let me go. I've got a dream, a mission, a reason to live!"

"Not anymore!" Eep said brightly.

Grug ignored Guy, hoisting the log onto his shoulder. He began to walk, and the Croods fell into step behind him. Guy's heart sank as he realized that Grug was walking away from the Mountain, right into the heart of danger.

"Um, I've got an idea," Guy said, thinking quickly. "Let's go to that Mountain."

He nodded toward a tall mountain far off in the distance.

Grug barely glanced at it. "It's too far," he said, and kept walking.

"Dad really has his heart set on a cave," Eep informed Guy.

"Uh, there are caves on that Mountain," Guy lied. Belt gave Guy a confused look, and Guy gave him a look in return that said, *Hey, come on, back me up*. This was the only way to get stubborn Grug to go in the right direction.

Eep was suspicious. "Have you been there?" she asked.

"It's a mountain," Guy replied. "Mountains are safe. Mountains have caves. And water. And sticks." He thought his argument sounded pretty good. And once they got to the Mountain, he could leave the Croods and see what was waiting on the other side.

Thunk was already excited. "Mom, did you hear that? I can get my own stick!"

Guy nodded, happy that he seemed to be getting through to the cavemen. "Yes. Sticks. Caves and sticks. Crazy sticks. Let's go!"

Grug stopped.

Guy had finally gotten his attention. The rest of the

60

Croods stared at Grug, waiting to see what he would do.

Then the earth began to rumble and shake again. The ground split in two over by a grove of trees, and a mammoth that had been peacefully munching on leaves was swallowed in an instant, vanishing into a gaping abyss.

Belt wiggled his eyebrows. "Da da daaaaa," the sloth chirped in an ominous tone.

It was the first time the other Croods had noticed Belt. Thunk made a face. "Ugh. That thing is weird."

Sandy buried her head in Ugga's shoulder, frightened.

"It's okay, Sandy," Eep assured her. "That's just a belt."

Grug took a step backward and turned to his family.

"I've made a decision," he announced. "We're going to that Mountain! Don't ask me why. It's just a hunch. It just feels right."

Ugga looked worried. "I don't know, Grug. We've never really walked that far."

"I don't think my feet can do that," Thunk chimed in.

"I'll never live long enough to get there," Gran complained.

That last comment made Grug happy. "Let's do it!" he said, more determined than ever. "Oh, come on, just think. Our whole family, packed together on a long, slow trip across the country? Days and nights with just each other? We'll tell stories. We'll laugh."

He glanced at Eep. "We'll become closer as a family."

Eep raised an eyebrow. Her dad was being such a . . . a *dad* lately. They'd lived together in a cave for years and years. It didn't get much closer than that, did it? So why did Grug keep pushing all the family stuff? The world was ending, the cave was gone, and Eep still couldn't get a break from her overprotective father.

The rest of the Croods weren't thrilled about taking the long journey to the Mountain, but Grug had made up his mind, and they knew there was no changing it.

"Let's go," Grug ordered, and one by one, they started following him toward the Mountain.

CHAPTER 8

The Croods hadn't walked for very long before they started feeling weary from their journey.

Grug carried the log containing Guy on his shoulder, and Ugga held Sandy in her arms, until the little girl got restless. As soon as she was free, she ran over to Thunk and started nipping at his arms and legs.

"Aah! Get her off! Get her off!" Thunk cried.

"If you're not ready to challenge her, then don't look her in the eye," Ugga said.

Thunk swatted Sandy away, and she scampered up next to Gran, who was yelling at Grug.

"Could you keep your big giant arms on your side of the trail?"

"No more touching. No more touching," Ugga pleaded, as Eep kept bumping into her as they walked.

"Isn't this fun? We're taking our first trip together," Eep said cheerfully.

But her smile faded when Thunk accidentally bumped into her. She spun around, her eyes blazing.

"Stop shoving, or I will pull out your tongue!"

Grug stopped short and turned to look at his family. "Do you want me to turn this family around? Do you? Because I will turn this family around so fast!"

The Croods were miserable, but Grug wasn't giving up. They kept on walking, traveling across a landscape that had been destroyed by earthquakes and fire. The beautiful, colorful Jungle was just a memory, and now they were surrounded by blackened, leafless trees.

The bleak surroundings didn't improve anyone's mood.

"Dad, I gotta go!" Thunk complained, doing a little dance.

"Come on, you can hold it," Grug said.

"I don't think so," Thunk said with a moan. "I gotta go really bad."

He started to hop around with his knees stuck together. Grug took pity on him.

"Go behind one of those lumpy things, and make it fast," Grug said with a sigh as he brought the family to a stop.

Thunk ran off toward one of the brown lumpy things Grug had pointed toward. They sort of looked like rocks, except they weren't. Poor Thunk had disturbed a sleeping creature—one with teeth.

"Ow! Something bit me!" Thunk cried.

"I don't blame it!" Gran shouted back.

Ugga had other worries. "Maybe we should have stopped for water," she said, as the hot sun beat down on them.

They got back on the trail, and Eep ran up next to her father.

"Dad, can I take a turn carrying him?" she asked.

"No," Grug replied firmly, without even looking at his daughter.

"How about now?" Eep asked.

"No."

"Now?" Eep asked.

"No."

Eep wasn't about to give up. "NOW?" she yelled.

"NO!" Grug yelled back.

Eep yelled again, even louder. "NOW?"

"I can do this all day long," Grug said, keeping his cool. "No, no, no, and still no."

Eep finally gave up and walked back to the end of the line. The Croods kept going and going, and the

Mountain didn't look any closer. Their moods weren't getting any better either. Their last meal of popcorn was a distant memory now, and their stomachs grumbled.

"I'm not dying on an empty stomach," Gran complained.

"Grug, we're all getting pretty tired," Ugga pointed out.

"I'm pretty dizzy, so I'm just going to lie down for a minute," Thunk said, collapsing on the ground.

"We'll eat when we get there," Grug said, determined not to stop until they reached the safety of a cave.

"It's taking too long!" Gran said, stomping her foot. "I'm grabbing a snack!"

She jumped up on Guy's log, trying to grab Belt, who had been keeping Guy company on the log. The sloth pulled out a knife made of bone to defend himself.

"No, no, no!" Guy warned, shaking his head. "Don't do that. He will cut you. That's not food, he's a pet. My pet."

Gran wrinkled her brow. "What's a pet?"

"An animal that you don't eat," Guy explained.

"We call those children," Gran informed him.

Grug frowned. "No man should have a pet. It's weird. And wrong. It's . . . food!"

"No, no, please!" Guy begged.

"Not that," Grug said. He pointed to an area of tall grass up ahead. "That."

A giant blue bird lifted its head. The brightly colored creature had a huge, long beak filled with sharp teeth. It was a Turkeyfish, and it looked delicious.

"Food fixes everything," Grug said confidently. He grabbed Thunk. "All right, son, show me your hunting face."

Thunk screwed up his face and growled. "Aargh!"

Eep wanted to hunt too, so she jumped in front of Grug and made her hunting face.

"Not you!" Grug yelled. "You're still grounded."

He lowered Thunk. "Come on, Thunk."

"My feet hurt," Thunk whined.

Guy led the rest of his family to a large boulder and instructed them to wait for him there. He propped Guy's log against the rock, next to Gran, Ugga, Sandy, and Eep.

Guy noticed that Eep was staring at Grug and Thunk as they went off after the bird.

"You look tense," Guy remarked.

"I'm not tense," Eep said crossly, but it was clear that she was.

Gran understood. "Angry girl wants to do what they're doing," she said, nodding toward the hunters.

Eep never understood why her dad even took Thunk hunting. He was hopeless! Right now he was stepping on every twig and leaf as he tried to sneak up on the bird.

The bird, of course, heard Thunk coming. His bright green eyes flashed angrily, and it wasn't long before he was the one doing the pursuing. Thunk screamed and ran away. Grug grabbed the bird's tail as he sped by, but he couldn't take down the big creature. Now the bird was dragging Grug across the ground behind him.

"Hang on, Thunk. I'm coming!" Grug tried to assure his son.

"Why are you doing this?" Thunk asked the Turkeyfish.

Guy looked at Eep, confused. "What are they doing?"

"Hunting," Ugga explained, but it didn't look like hunting to Guy. The bird had picked up Thunk in his beak and began thrashing the boy back and forth.

"Get it off!" Thunk wailed.

"No, seriously," Guy said to Ugga. "What are they doing?"

"Get off, get off!" Thunk begged the bird. "You've got a ton of eggs. Just make another egg!"

The bird tossed Thunk, slamming him into a giant

Brontoscorpion on a rock. Thunk and the bug slid down to the ground. Then the bird hopped up on a rock and jumped on top of Thunk like a wrestler leaping from the top rope onto his opponent.

"Now you're just rubbing it in," Thunk complained.

After the bird was done with Thunk, Grug brought the Brontoscorpion that Thunk had smashed back to the rest of the Croods. The creature had six wiggling legs and a spearlike tail.

"There, food fixes everything!" Grug said proudly. "Now, eat up before it stops wiggling!"

The hungry Croods pulled at the legs, eating the bug like they were chowing down on the world's most delectable dish. Guy looked nauseous.

"What happened to the egg and the bird?" he asked.

"You know, we lost it," Thunk said, as bug juice dripped down his chin. "But when the bird stepped on me and pushed me into the ground, the scorpion grabbed ahold of me, and one thing led to another and here we are, eating him. Win-win." He grinned.

Within minutes there was hardly anything left of the scorpion.

"Not enough. Not enough," Gran complained. "I need more. I need more!" She turned to Guy with a hungry look in her eyes.

"Oh, look at that," Guy said nervously. "She's not gonna eat me, right?"

"You're too skinny," Ugga replied. "If she was going to eat anyone, it would be—"

"Aaaaaaaah!" Thunk yelled. Gran had chomped down on his arm like it was a piece of chicken. He tried to pry her off, but she wouldn't budge. "Oww! She's locked her jaw!"

"Mom!" Ugga cried.

"Someone get a stick! Get her off!" Thunk wailed desperately. He kept swatting at Gran, but she was like a rabid beast, mad with hunger, and wouldn't let go. Guy watched, horrified, while Sandy ran off to find a stick.

"Oh, you sick old monster!" Thunk moaned, but he was relieved when Sandy scampered up with the stick. "Hurry! Put the stick in her mouth!"

"Hold her still," Grug instructed. "Use a rock. Ugga, would you just hit her legs?"

Back in the log, Belt looked at Guy and squeaked. The Croods were distracted. This would be the perfect time to escape.

Guy was stuck tightly in the log, but he was able to get it moving by rolling across the ground. He rolled away as quickly as he could until the sound of the arguing Croods was far behind him.

70

Suddenly the log stopped rolling. Guy looked up to see Eep pinning down the log with her foot.

"Why are you rolling away?" she asked.

"I just want something to eat!" Guy wailed, exasperated.

"You had bug for dinner. Plenty of bug!" Eep told him.

Guy had an idea. "Please," he said. "I'll let you help me hunt."

Eep raised an eyebrow. "Really?"

She started to help him out of the log. Behind them, they could still hear Thunk screaming for his life.

CHAPTER 9

Guy stretched, feeling the warm sun on his arms. It felt good to be out of that log! Now he just needed some food. He had a very different approach to hunting from the Croods.

First he took a long rope from his pouch. He walked to the base of a tree with a round trunk and spiky branches, and tied the rope to it. He pointed to the top of the tree.

Eep understood. She jumped up to the top of the tree, and the thin tree trunk bent down until it touched the ground. Guy took over, tying a loop in the end of the rope.

"What do you call this?" Eep asked, watching his every move curiously.

"A trap," Guy explained.

Eep was more curious than ever. Everything Guy did was new and exciting. "What does it do?"

Guy tried to act it out for her. He walked over by the trap and whistled. Then he pretended to be the big Turkeyfish bird, stomping across the terrain. Then he mimicked the bird's leg getting caught in the trap, and then hoisted in the air when the bent tree branch snapped back up.

"Ta-daa!" he said when he was finished.

"How long have you been alone?" Eep asked when Guy was done with his pantomime.

Belt opened his arms wide, and Eep understood—Guy had been alone for a long, long time.

"So what do we do now?" Eep asked.

Guy pulled something else out of his pouch. It looked like a small Turkeyfish bird, but Eep realized it was a doll of some kind that Guy must have made.

"How's your acting?" he said with a grin.

He motioned for Eep to follow him to a rock just past the snare. They crouched behind the rock, and Guy showed her that the doll was really a puppet. Guy used his hands to work the puppet's head and wings, and Eep worked the legs and tail.

Eep giggled as she and Guy made the puppet do a silly dance. Guy started to whistle again and peeked around the rock. He could see the Turkeyfish in the distance, slowly approaching them.

"You're good at this," he told Eep.

They had so much fun working the puppet that the dance got wilder and wilder. They quickly got tangled up.

"Just move your arm . . . no, your other arm," Eep said, trying to get free. "Oh, wait, that one's my arm!"

They didn't realize it, but they had turned the puppet completely around, and it shook its tail feathers at the approaching Turkeyfish—a huge insult if you are a Turkeyfish. Furious, the bird jumped clear across Guy's trap and landed on the rock, snatching the puppet right from their hands. He swung his beak back and forth, angrily thrashing the puppet against the rocks.

"Uh, it didn't step on your trap-y thing," Eep pointed out.

"Yeah, I noticed," Guy said sarcastically.

The giant bird hopped off the rock and faced Eep and Guy, ready to attack. Eep bravely took a stance in front of the huge creature, but he lunged for Guy first. He grabbed him with his beak and tossed him across the field. He went flying through the air, screaming— and landed right back inside the log.

Grug's head snapped around when he heard the commotion.

"Where's Eep?" he asked Guy.

Guy didn't need to answer, because at that moment Eep raced past, chased by the giant Turkeyfish.

"She's awesome," Guy said admiringly.

Grug raced toward the tree. "Eep!"

Eep saw that he was about to step right into Guy's trap. "Dad, no!"

Guy thought quickly. He rolled up to Grug and kicked him as hard as he could. Grug went down, missing the snare.

Then Eep took over, running right toward the trap with the bird still chasing her. She effortlessly jumped over it . . . but this time, the Turkeyfish stepped right into it.

The bird hit the trigger and caught his foot in the loop of rope. He lunged forward, angrily snapping at Guy, Grug, and Eep with his sharp beak, but before he could make contact, the bent tree snapped back.

Boing! The bird whooshed backward into the air, soaring way up into the sky. Then he crashed down into the field, sending a shower of colorful feathers into the air. Success!

Not long after, the Croods were sitting around an open fire, roasting the giant bird. Guy sat with them, his ankle roped to a heavy rock. He had finished his dinner and was now anxiously watching the Croods. He had never seen people eat so much!

Thunk licked the juices from his lips. "It's an avalanche of flavor!" he raved. The Croods rarely ate meat, and when they did, it was always raw. Cooked was way more delicious.

The rest of the family, including Sandy, was chomping on the barbecued bird like a pack of hungry wolves. When a scrap fell from a bone, they fought with one another to see who would grab it.

Finally satisfied, Eep walked over to Guy and sat next to him. He and Belt were looking at each other, shaking their heads.

"Looks like we won't have any leftovers," Guy said glumly.

"What are leftovers?" Eep asked.

Guy was confused. Didn't everyone know that? "You know, when you have so much food to eat you have some left over."

Eep shook her head. "That never happens to us."

Grug overheard their conversation, and it bothered him. Guy's fancy trap had provided the family with a delicious meal, and what had Grug provided? One big, slimy bug. And Guy wasn't even big and strong! For the first time in his life, Grug was filled with doubt that he

Grug signals to his family. Time to find breakfast!

Sandy scampers out of the cave.

Eep tells the sun to come back tomorrow.

Grug tells his family a story. It's a warning not to do anything new or different . . . or they could end up like Krispy Bear!

There's a light in the dark night.
What could it be?

Eep discovers fire for the first time
and is fascinated.

The ground starts to shake!
Grug must protect his family!

The cave is gone! The Croods enter a
colorful New World.

The Croods encounter many strange creatures, like Punch Monkeys.

Guy uses his fire to save them from a swarm of Piranhakeets.

Thunk thought fire
was his friend,
until it started
"biting" him!

The Croods light a giant corn field on fire.
Popcorn for everyone!

Guy joins the Croods' family road trip—whether he wants to or not.

The Croods—the family that sticks together, survives together.

could take care of his family. And if he couldn't do that, then what good was he?

Ugga noticed his troubled expression.

"Grug, how about a story?" she suggested. She knew that telling a story would cheer him up.

It worked. "That's a good idea," Grug agreed. "How about a story, huh?"

"Yeah, a story! Tell us a story!" Thunk cried, still hyped up on meat.

The Croods gathered around Grug. He gazed around the circle and went into his best storytelling voice.

"Once upon a time there was a little tiger who lived in a cave with her family," he said, glancing at Eep. "There were a lot of rules, but the big, simple one was to never leave the cave at night. And the door was so heavy, you'd think it would be easy to remember."

"So easy to remember!" Thunk chimed in, and Eep rolled her eyes. She knew where this was headed.

"I know!" Grug agreed. "But while everyone was asleep, she went out anyway."

"No!" exclaimed Ugga, Thunk, and Gran, horrified. Eep just kept scowling.

"Yes!" Grug said. "And no sooner than she did her cave was destroyed and everyone had to go on this long, stinky walk, with some weirdo they met, and died! The end."

Everyone except Eep and Guy gasped in terror.

"Whoa! I did not see that coming," Guy said sincerely. "Twist ending. My stories never end like that."

Thunk pumped his fist in the air. "Yes! Two stories in one night!"

He moved over to Guy, and the rest of the Croods followed. Grug was in shock. *He* was the family storyteller! He always had been. Why was everybody so crazy about this Guy guy?

"Okay, but it won't be as good as Grug's," Guy said carefully. He didn't want to hurt Grug's feelings . . . or make him angry! "Um, once upon a time, there was a beautiful tiger. She lived in a cave with the rest of her family. Her father and mother told her, 'You may go anywhere you want, but never go near the cliff, for you could fall.'"

"And die," Grug interrupted. "Good story."

But Guy wasn't finished.

"But when no one was looking, she would go near the cliff, for the closer she came to the edge, the more she could hear, the more she could see, and the more she could feel."

Eep listened, wide-eyed. She knew Guy's story was

for her. It was like he knew exactly how she had been feeling inside all these years.

"Finally she stood at the very edge, and she saw a light," Guy went on, and the Croods listened intently. "She leaned to touch it, and slipped."

Grug knew how this story would end. "And she fell," he finished.

"And she *flew*," Guy corrected him.

The rest of the family gasped. They had never heard a story like this before!

"Where did she fly?" asked Thunk.

"Tomorrow," Guy said.

Eep frowned. "Tomorrow?"

"A place with more suns in the sky than you can count," Guy said.

Thunk's dark eyes sparkled as he imagined it. "It would be so bright."

"A place not like today, or yesterday," Guy continued. "A place where things are better."

Grug snorted. "Tomorrow isn't a place. You can't see it!"

"Oh, yes it is," Guy assured him. "I've seen it. That's where I'm going."

Grug studied Guy's face carefully. The boy looked sincere, but he sounded crazy. Then Grug looked at

Eep, who looked entranced by Guy, and Grug started feeling annoyed all over again.

"Well, *we* are going to shut our eyes and sleep," Grug said firmly. "And when we wake up, we're going to find the place that has everything we want."

"Tomorrow?" Eep asked, thinking of the beautiful land Guy had described.

"A cave," Grug said flatly.

He got up, untied Guy, and stuffed him neatly back inside the log. Then he curled up by the fire with Guy tucked under his arm.

The rest of the Croods curled up too. With their bellies full of food and their heads full of stories, they drifted off into a peaceful sleep.

Grug was the only one who didn't sleep peacefully. He tossed and turned, worried about his family. He finally drifted off as the morning light rose over the horizon.

Guy was the first to open his eyes—and what he saw terrified him. There had been another earthquake during the night. The Croods were safe, but the quake had split the ground in two, and Guy's log was dangling over a two-hundred-foot-deep abyss!

"Aaaaaaah!" he screamed.

CHAPTER 10

Guy's scream woke up the Croods, who quickly realized what had happened. Grug pulled Guy to safety and then ordered the others to get on their feet. It was time to move out again.

Grug tried not to show it, but his confidence was at its lowest point. The family had just escaped death, no thanks to him. He wasn't going to take any more chances. Holding Guy in the log again, he led his family to the Mountain, testing each step himself before he would let anyone else proceed. The whole process was painstakingly slow.

"That was too close," Guy said to Eep. He was still shaken. "It almost caught us."

"I was watching. We were fine," Grug said, but he didn't really believe his own words.

"Well, we've got to move faster," Guy urged. "Do you people have any other speed aside from 'wander'? I'll take 'shamble' at this point."

"Hey, do you have a minute?" Eep asked Guy. "How did the tiger fly?"

"I only share when I'm outside the log," Guy replied. "I'm funny that way."

Eep winked at him. "Leave this to me."

She fell back in line behind Thunk, so that her brother was right behind Grug.

"Hey, Thunk, you have a spider on your face," Eep lied. Then she grabbed Gran's cane and whacked Thunk on the back of the head. He knocked into Grug, sending Guy and the log flying. Grug looked behind him and gave Eep an annoyed look. He knew what she was up to.

"Oops," Eep said innocently.

Guy's log rolled away from the Croods onto a wide field of coral that lay between the Croods and the Mountain. The field had held an ocean once, long before the earthquakes, but now the water was gone, and all that remained were seashells and a bed of sharp, pointy coral.

"He's loose!" Grug yelled, chasing after Guy. But when he stepped onto the Coral Field, he cried out in pain. "Aaah! Do not step on those weird, pointy rocks!"

"You mean these rocks?" Thunk asked, running after him right onto the coral. "Ah! Ow! Do not step on those rocks!"

Gran pushed between Ugga and Eep. "Step aside, girls," she said, running onto the Coral Field. But just like Grug and Thunk, as soon as Gran's feet stomped on the coral, she cried out in pain.

"Hello? Nobody's listening!" Grug fumed. "You cannot walk on those!"

Meanwhile, Guy was able to shatter the log and free himself. He could stand on the coral without any problem, because he wore shoes on his feet. This was his chance to escape. Grug spotted Guy darting away.

"Come back here now!" Grug bellowed. He tried to run after Guy but had to stop when he stepped on a sharp piece of coral.

"Well, there goes our chance for survival," Gran said dismally.

Thunk picked up a piece of the log. "And our log!" he wailed.

But Guy hadn't run away, not yet. He had taken refuge behind a giant clamshell.

Sure, the Croods had kept him prisoner in a log and ate bugs and were dangerous around fire. But they were starting to grow on him. He felt a stab of pity as they tried to make their way across the field.

"Ow!" Thunk cried. "Jumping doesn't help. I mean, just briefly, but it doesn't get any better!"

He tried another tactic, flipping over and walking on his hands. "Ow! Do not walk on your hands! The hands do not help at all!"

Guy looked toward the Mountain, which was so close now that he still had hope he could reach it in time. Then he looked back at the Croods again. What should he do?

Belt helped him make up his mind. He hopped off Guy and pulled him by the hand, back toward the Croods.

"Eeecooommme on!" Belt squeaked.

As he walked, Guy picked up some things that he knew would help the Croods. He appeared back at the start of the Coral Field, his arms full. As soon as he saw Guy, Grug quickly picked up another log.

"I can help you, but we're going to have to make a few changes," Guy said. "The log ride is over. Drop the log."

Grug grudgingly dropped it.

"Now kick it away," Guy instructed.

Grug nudged it with his big toe.

"Farther," Guy said.

Grug knew when he'd been beaten. He gave the log a good kick, sending it sailing across the Coral Field.

"Okay, smart Guy," Grug said. "Now what?"

A short time later the Croods made their way across the Coral Field without yelling in pain. Guy had constructed a crude pair of shoes for everyone, but the Croods were terrified of them. Who ever heard of wearing things on your feet?

Thunk slowly plodded along the field with his eyes closed. He was so afraid of his shoes that he couldn't look at them. Finally he braved a quick peek. His feet were stuffed into two huge fish with bulging eyes. They blinked at Thunk, and he let out a scream.

Guy wanted to surprise Eep, so he made her close her eyes while he fixed her shoes on her feet.

"Okay, now you can look," he said when he was finished.

Eep looked down to see two pretty pink starfish covering her feet.

"Aaaaah, I love them!" she cried. "But where are my feet?"

"They're still there," Guy assured her.

"Oh, okay," Eep said. It was hard to believe. She took her first, tentative step and slipped, falling into Guy's arms. They both fell down on the coral.

"Wow, you're really . . . heavy," he said, trying to push her back up.

"Really? Thank you!" Eep said, pleased.

Grug saw Eep and Guy on the ground and broke into a run. He had to break that up, and fast! But he wasn't used to his new shoes, and he lost his footing and slipped.

"Okay, she's up," Guy said, getting back on his feet. "I'm good. We're good."

Ugga and Gran were having better luck with the shoes, and they quickly got the hang of walking in them.

"These shoes are great!" Gran said. "Where do you get these ideas?"

"Aha," Guy replied, pleased that she had asked. As if on cue, Belt produced a piece of chalk. Guy grabbed Thunk and propped him up next to a flat wall of rock. Then Guy stood next to Thunk, and Belt outlined them both.

When Belt was done, Guy took the chalk and drew a circle inside the outline of his head, but left Thunk's head empty.

"I'm calling it a brain," Guy explained. "I'm pretty sure it's where ideas come from."

Thunk looked sad. "Dad, I don't have a brain."

Grug was annoyed. "We've gotten along just fine without brains until now," he said. "Cavemen don't need brains. We have these!" He balled up his mighty fists and punched the air. "Hee-ya! Hee-ya! That's what I'm talking about! Ideas are for weaklings!" Grug cried triumphantly. "Now let's get to that Mountain."

The Croods started walking again. As Eep reached her mom, they both looked down and admired each other's shoes. "I love those!" they both said at once.

Thunk was a little less in love with his shoes. "Good fish," he told them. "Don't eat my feet."

CHAPTER II

The Croods crossed the Coral Field slowly at first, but once they got used to the shoes they began to run—fast! Eep grabbed Guy's hand and practically dragged him across the field.

As the day went on, the Coral Field gave way to more dense Jungle. A group of chattering Punch Monkeys swung down from the trees, blocking their way.

Grug balled his hands into fists, ready for them this time. "Yeah? You want a go? Stand back. This is going to get ugly."

But Guy had a different plan. He walked up to the monkeys, handing out bananas. "And one for you, and one for you, and one for you," he said, and the satisfied monkeys grabbed them and swung away. Guy gave the last one to Grug. "And one for you!"

Grug scowled and tossed the banana away.

After they passed through the Jungle, the group came to a rocky plain. A wide canyon stretched across the plain, too wide to jump across. But Guy had a plan for that, too. He hiked to the tree line and made stilts for everyone out of tall branches. The Croods looked nervously at the stilts.

"Come on. Keep it moving. The Mountain is not going to grow legs and come to us," he urged.

One by one the Croods planted the bottom of the stilts in the bottom of the canyon and slowly walked across like circus performers. Guy took the lead, and Grug brought up the rear.

Eep was still thinking about Guy's story.

"So, how did the tiger fly?" she asked him again.

This time Guy had an answer for her. "He jumped on the sun and rode it to Tomorrow."

Eep looked up at the sky, at the round yellow sun burning brightly there. Could you really jump on it? The top of the Mountain was closer now, and she tried to imagine jumping from the mountaintop onto the sun, and then flying away. . . . It was a thrilling thought, and it spurred her to move even faster.

Grug trailed behind all of them, unsteady on the stilts. He looked down and saw Chunky, the fierce

Macawnivore, at the bottom of the canyon. Thankfully, the sleeping cat didn't seem to notice the seven tasty meals passing by overhead.

Grug tried to move around the beast, but he unintentionally whacked Chunky in the face with one of his stilts. Startled, the Macawnivore swiped a paw at the strange moving sticks. His sharp claws sliced right through them, chopping off a chunk of the stilts. Grug's stomach lurched as he dropped down by a good three feet.

Grug tried to hurry across the canyon now, but the Macawnivore was fascinated with the sticks and took another swipe at them.

Whack! Grug dropped down again. He kept moving, still trying to reach the other side of the canyon.

Whack!

Whack!

Whack!

The Macawnivore sliced away until Grug reached the bottom of the canyon, face-to-face with the fierce creature.

On the other side of the cliff, the other Croods and Guy listened as Chunky and Grug fought each other below.

Grug finally escaped the snarling Macawnivore and

scrambled up the side of the canyon to join his family. They walked some more until they came to another obstacle—the top of a steep cliff.

As usual, Grug tried to take charge.

"Step where I step," he ordered his family. He lowered himself down to a ledge, holding on to the jagged cliff side with his strong arms.

And, as usual, Guy had an idea for a better way to do it.

"Uh, we don't have time for this," he said. He found a nearby tree with giant, round leaves and picked one for himself and each Crood. Then he sat on his leaf and inched close to the edge of the cliff. He pushed himself off, using the leaf to slide down.

"Come on!" Guy called behind him.

Everyone except for Grug grabbed a leaf and pushed off, gleefully sliding down the cliff side.

"Eat my leaf!" Gran yelled as she picked up speed.

Eep whizzed by her father, who was still carefully climbing down.

"Dad!" she called out, but Grug wasn't interested in any of Guy's ideas.

Thunk zipped up to Grug next. "Hi, Dad!" he yelled as he approached. And then, "Bye, Dad!"

Grug stumbled and fell, landing at the bottom of the

cliff with his family. He stood up and dusted himself off, planning to lecture them about the dangers of sliding down things, when . . .

BOOM! Thunder rumbled in the canyon, and a flash of lightning blazed in the sky. The Croods looked up to see huge, purple storm clouds surrounding them in every direction. And then it started to rain.

The Croods froze, dumbstruck.

"It's just rain," Guy said. "You've seen rain before?"

"We don't get out much," Eep explained.

The rain poured down on them. Grug thought of each and every drop as an enemy, and he started punching them. Guy, of course, had another idea.

He took an umbrella made of sticks and an animal hide out of his pouch. He opened it, and Belt pulled Eep inside with them.

"Why do you know so much about Tomorrow?" Eep asked.

"Because that's where I'm going," Guy said confidently.

Grug stopped punching raindrops and swiftly pulled the umbrella away from Guy. He started to do a little victory dance when . . . *wham!* A streak of lightning hit him.

The fast, heavy rain quickly filled the canyon they

had slid down into, creating a natural swimming pool. The Croods were stuck on an island in the middle of it. Eep was mesmerized by what she saw in the water . . . her reflection.

"Hello," she said to herself.

Grug didn't like it. "Looks dangerous," he told his daughter.

But Eep was used to that attitude from her dad. "Oh, Dad, you say that about everything." She decided she wanted to join the other Eep in the water. She was about to jump in when Guy stopped her.

"Careful," he told her, and then he cannonballed into the water.

When he emerged, he told Eep to follow him. She jumped into the water, but she didn't know how to swim. Luckily, Guy was willing to teach her.

"Relax," he told her as he held her up in the water. Soon Eep was swimming.

Gran and Ugga smiled at each other. Swimming looked like so much fun!

Splash! Gran, Ugga, Sandy, and Thunk jumped in at the same time and began splashing and swimming. Grug stayed on the rock, his arms stubbornly folded across his chest.

Belt climbed up on Grug's arm and jumped off it

like it was a diving board. Gran, Sandy, and Belt began swimming back and forth in time, moving like synchronized swimmers.

Eep dove under the water and emerged with Guy riding on her shoulders. That sight was enough to finally get Grug off the rock.

"No, no, no! Not cool! Not cool!" he fumed, and then he dove in.

A huge wave splashed up when Grug hit the water. It knocked Guy off Eep's shoulders, like he wanted, but Grug sank to the bottom like a rock.

Above him, Guy and the other Croods had grabbed the tails of some big, friendly Fish Cats and were letting the spotted, whiskered fish pull them around the water. Grug saw them overhead, but right now his spirits were as low as the canyon floor. His family no longer needed him. Guy was smart. Guy was fun. Guy had a brain thing that gave him ideas. He might as well stay here at the bottom of the water forever.

A big bubble escaped Grug's nose as he held his breath. His eyes followed the bubble as it floated to the surface—and that was when he saw the Macawnivore swimming toward him. That got Grug moving, fast.

Grug might have been down, but he wasn't out. Not yet, anyway.

CHAPTER 12

Swimming was fun, but Guy knew they didn't have time to waste. Once the travelers made their way across the water, they started walking toward the Mountain again, and everyone—except for Grug—was in a great mood.

"So the bear says, 'Your cave? I've been dumping my bones here since last week,'" Guy said.

"Last week, ha!" Gran laughed. "That's a funny story!"

"It's not a story, it's a joke," Guy explained.

"What's a joke?" Gran asked.

"You know . . . just making something up, to make you laugh," Guy explained.

Gran laughed again. "Ha! Don't get it."

They soon came to an open plain deeply furrowed

with winding grooves that formed one giant maze. To cross the plain, the Croods would have to walk through the curves of the Maze.

Guy had a plan to get through the Maze quickly. He handed out shells to each of the Croods.

"Here you go," he said. "One for you, and one for you . . ."

Bwaaaaaap! Everyone except for Grug began blowing into their shells loudly.

"Okay, okay!" Grug snapped, annoyed. "I don't see why the kids need their own shells."

"So if anyone gets in trouble, we can call the others," Guy said.

Grug's eyebrows shot up. "Wait—you're saying we should split up?"

"We can try more paths at once," Guy explained. "It's the fastest way through."

As if on cue, the earth beneath their feet began to rumble gently, reminding them that they needed to hurry. But Grug didn't care.

"Croods stick together," he said firmly. "Your way isn't safe."

"They can handle it," Guy insisted.

"We can do it, Dad," Eep piped up.

Grug shook his head. "No, no, no, no, no. It's my job

to keep you safe. I'm still in charge, and we are not split-ting up."

He looked at Eep and Guy, who were standing together. "Except for you two. And that's final."

Grug sat down, determined not to move until he got his way. But then he felt the earth start to move once more.

This rumble was big—earth-breaking big. The ground shook violently, and the force knocked every-one to the ground. They slid into the grooves of the Maze, each of them landing in a different path.

Finally the shaking stopped. Everyone stood up and got a look at their surroundings. A feeling of alarm rose in Grug when he realized that he was separated from the others.

"Hello? Is everyone all right?" he asked, frightened.

"We're okay, Grug!" Ugga called out, trying to keep him calm. She had Sandy in one arm, and Gran was by her side.

Thunk wasn't calm at all. "Dad? I'm freaking out a little bit. Just tell me what to do."

"Stay where you are," Grug replied. "I'll find you."

"No!" Guy yelled. "Too slow. Everybody, keep mov-ing forward and we'll get out."

Grug growled. There was Guy, giving the orders

again. But the young stranger was probably right.

"Dad?" Thunk asked.

"Yeah. Okay," Grug replied, trying not to lose his cool. "Remember, never *not* be afraid."

Guy tried something more reassuring. "You can do this!"

"It's gonna be okay," Thunk said. "I'm gonna pass out."

But he didn't. He picked up his shell, which he had dropped during his fall, and made his way through the passage. There was blue sky above him, and nothing but more passageway ahead of him, but at least he knew his dad was on the other side of those walls.

Everyone moved forward as quickly as they could, following the twists and turns of the Maze.

Gran and Ugga turned right and walked right into several big flowers with sharp, snapping teeth.

Thunk kept walking and came face-to-face with a Crocopup, a chubby creature with a long, reptilian mouth filled with sharp teeth, a furry body, and wagging tail.

Eep found a beautiful blue flower that had dropped right in the middle of her path. Who could have thrown it there?

And Grug stood at a fork in his path, scratching his

head and wondering if he should go left or right.

Guy wasn't telling the Croods what to do, but one by one they figured it out.

Gran and Ugga decorated themselves with lots of regular flowers and snuck past the carnivorous flowers easily in their disguise.

Afraid, Thunk threw his shell at the Crocopup, but he missed. To his surprise, the creature fetched it, brought it back to Thunk, and dropped it at his feet. Thunk smiled. Then he tossed a rock, and the Crocopup went after it. Thunk ran after him.

Eep put the blue flower in her hair and kept walking. Next she found a tiny pink shell in her path and picked it up. Something told her that it wasn't there by accident. She ran off, looking for Guy.

Grug finally made a decision and chose a direction—only to find himself right back where he'd started.

Moving on instinct, Eep located Guy in a rainy grove of red trees. She shyly approached him and dropped the shell and flower in his hand.

"You dropped these," she said, smiling, and then quickly darted away.

Eep's next turn brought her to the end of the Maze. She found herself at the edge of a forest filled with huge redwood trees. In the distance, she could see the setting sun about to touch the very top of the Mountain. She held up her hand, making a bridge between the mountaintop and the sun. It was easy to imagine walking across it and disappearing into the bright light.

Guy exited the Maze right after Eep, and the first thing he noticed was the setting sun too. He held up his hand, just like Eep, and from the corner of his eye he saw that Eep was doing the exact same thing. Smiling, he walked to her and took her hand.

"Come with me," he whispered.

Eep turned and looked into Guy's eyes—just as her little brother emerged from the Maze. He tossed the rock again and the Crocopup waddled out of the Maze, chasing it.

"Here, boy, catch!" Thunk yelled.

Next, a loud shell blared from inside the Maze as Ugga, Gran, and Sandy came out of it. They were still covered in their flower camouflage.

"Gran?" asked Thunk, not sure who was behind all those petals.

"Mom?" asked Eep.

They shook off the flowers as three more shell blasts erupted from somewhere inside the Maze. Ugga turned to face the tunnel and cupped her hands around her mouth.

100

"Grug?" she called out.

Another blast from the shell answered her.

Ugga sighed. "I'll go get him."

Grug blew his shell one more time and then sat down, defeated. This was all because of Guy! They could be safe and sound in some cave somewhere, but *noooooo*, they had to listen to Guy. Guy and his "Tomorrow." Grug didn't even know if it was real.

But there was one thing he did know. There was no room for Grug in Guy's Tomorrow.

101

CHAPTER 13

Ugga and Grug finally escaped the Maze and followed the sound of laughter to a giant redwood tree in the middle of the Forest. Grug looked up to see swinging hammocks, flaming torches, and his family all gathered around Guy in a cozy crook of the tree. What was his family doing all the way up there? That wasn't safe at all!

"Come down here! Croods!" he yelled in a panic.

Ugga placed a hand on his shoulder. "Grug, they're okay. Guy's with them."

Those words didn't exactly comfort Grug. "Oh, oh, Guy. *Guy* is with them," he said, and it was obvious his feelings were hurt. "Well, thanks for bringing me that interesting Guy update!"

Ugga studied her husband's face. She knew he was

hurting, but right now he was acting more like a child than the leader of a caveman clan.

"I'm going to join our family," she said. "You can join me when you're ready."

But Grug was having none of it. "Sleep pile?" he called up. "How about a story, huh? Anyone?" Nobody answered.

That was because the Croods and Guy were having a great time.

Guy had lit some torches. Gran relaxed in a hammock made from a big leaf. Belt mixed up some fruit drinks in cups made from large, empty nutshells. Thunk played games with his new pet.

"Good boy," he told the Crocopup, who was splayed out on his back as Thunk scratched his belly. "Who's my good boy? You need a name? You want a name? I'm going to call you . . . Douglas!"

Thunk turned to Eep and Guy, beaming. "Look at him!" Then back to the Crocopup. "Can you do tricks? Roll over," he coaxed. "Come on, Douglas. Roll over."

The Crocopup obeyed—and rolled right out of the tree.

"Good boy, Douglas!" Thunk called down to the Forest floor.

Belt poured a drink for Gran and handed it to her.

"I was in love once," she was saying, with a dreamy look on her face. "He was a hunter. I was a gatherer. It was quite a scandal. We fed each other berries. We danced. Then my father smashed him with a rock and traded me to your grandfather."

Sandy and Belt both thought this was hilarious and collapsed into giggles.

A little while later, Gran, Belt, Sandy, and Thunk sat around a torch, watching bugs circle it. One of the bugs flew too close and . . . *ZAP!* The charred bug fell into Gran's lap.

"One point for me!" Gran cried, as Thunk, Sandy, and Belt laughed. Then Belt scratched a mark next to a drawing of Gran on the tree trunk. Each of the players had a little pile of charred, dead bugs next to them.

Ugga smiled and looked at Guy.

"They're crazy, but they have such good hearts," she told him. "I know it was hard for you to bring us along, but they had the best day of their lives. Thank you for that."

Before Guy could respond, they heard a low rumble in the distance. Guy looked to the horizon, worried. Fire and smoked erupted from the place they had just walked on earlier that day.

Eep came over to Guy, who then turned to the others.

"Follow me," he told them, and they began to climb.

What none of them knew was that Grug had snuck up the tree and followed too.

When the Croods got to the very top of the tree, Guy blew out his torch. When their eyes adjusted to the dark, they saw an amazing spectacle overhead, above the canopy leaves.

The night sky surrounded them, a black background filled with millions and millions of bright, shining stars. The Croods had never seen such a sight.

"More suns in the sky than you can count," Thunk said in awe.

"Every sun that crosses our sky comes to rest up there," Guy informed him.

Eep nodded. "Tomorrow."

"That's where we'll be safe," Guy promised.

Eep turned and looked at her family. "I'm going with Guy. Come with us."

Grug was hiding in the shadow of a branch, and Eep's words stung him worse than the bite of a Piranhakeet. He had already lost his cave, his old life, everything he had ever known . . . but losing Eep? He couldn't bear to think of it.

Ugga looked worried. "I can't go without Grug. I won't," she said.

"Well, that makes one of us," Gran piped up. "Count me in!"

Ugga couldn't believe her mother's betrayal. "Mom! Really? Now?"

"Grug has no idea how to protect us," Gran explained. "In fact, he has no ideas at all."

"That's not true," Ugga said, quickly jumping to her husband's defense—but then she faltered. "There was that one time he . . . uh . . ."

"Face it! If he actually had an idea of his own, I'd have a heart attack and die!" Gran said harshly.

Maybe it was the thought of losing Eep. Maybe it was the thought of losing his wife's confidence. Maybe it was the hope of finally getting rid of Gran. Or maybe it was all those reasons.

Something sparked inside of Grug. He wasn't going to give up. His family was following Guy because Guy had such great ideas, right? Well, he could have ideas too.

CHAPTER 14

Exhausted from the day's journey, the Croods all fell into a deep sleep in the safety of the tree. When Ugga woke up the next morning, she climbed down out of the tree and began to prepare for what she was going to say to Grug. She held Belt in her hand. He would help coach her for the hard task at hand.

"Face it, we've all changed, Grug," she practiced. "We're going to Tomorrow with Guy."

Belt shook his head.

"Too strong?" Ugga asked. She began again. "Grug, caveboy—" She sighed. "That was weird."

But Belt shook his head again.

"Is 'caveboy' too weird?" Ugga asked him.

Soon she walked out of the Forest. In front of her, she saw Grug. His back was to her.

"We need to talk, Grug," she said.

Grug turned around. "Haven't seen him."

Ugga screamed. Her husband was wearing the ugliest thing she'd ever seen. And it was on his head!

Soon the entire family had gathered around Grug.

"What are you doing?" Ugga asked her husband.

"Yeah, wow," said Grug, trying to sound cool. His eyes had that shiny look of someone who was losing it. "Like, I've been up all night. All these *ideas* kept coming to me."

Grug lifted his tunic. There was a boa constrictor around his waist!

"Is that a snake?" Guy asked in disbelief.

"Belt! New and improved! It's even self-tightening," Grug replied, but the snake kept tightening itself. A little too tight. Grug began to turn blue from lack of air. He smacked the snake, and it let loose a bit.

"What's that on your head?" Ugga asked next.

"It's called desperation," Gran quipped.

Grug ignored her and moved his fingers through the long strands on his head. "I call it a 'rug,'" he said, swinging his hair from side to side. "Rhymes with Grug. And this one—" He pointed to a huge rock next to him, which he had carved into the rough shape of, well, a car! "I call it a 'ride.' Rhymes with Grug!"

"That doesn't—" Guy began, but Grug interrupted him.

"It's gonna get us places faster than shoes," Grug promised. He hopped up on the rock. "Try to keep up."

Grug leaned forward, and the rock started to slide down a hill, quickly picking up speed. Grug couldn't control it.

Bam! It smashed through a tree, toppling it.

Only Thunk thought it was cool. "I wish *I* had a ride!"

Grug didn't let the crash stop him. He came back to the tree and slathered red mud all over his son.

"Painting is a thing of the past," he explained. "I call this a 'snapshot.'"

Grug took a big, flat stone and smashed it right into the boy. When he pulled the stone away, there was a red clay image of Thunk on the stone.

"Let's do it again," Thunk said. "I think I blinked."

And then he fainted.

The only one who liked this invention was Belt, who grabbed a rock to get his own snapshot of Thunk. He was about to throw it at the boy's face when Guy stopped him.

Grug handed out his next invention to his family— sunglasses made from wood, with solid wood lenses.

"I call them 'shades,'" Grug explained.

"The sun doesn't hurt my eyes anymore!" Thunk exclaimed, impressed.

That's because you can't see anything, Guy thought, but he kept his comment to himself.

Grug and Thunk began to stroll around in their new shades.

"Dad, where do you get these great ideas?" Thunk asked.

Grug's massive chest pumped up with pride. "Since I don't have a brain, they're coming from my stomach," he explained. "Down deep below, and then up again into my mind. My higher thoughts."

As Grug finished, Thunk walked right into a tree. *Bam!* The Croods took off their shades to see what had happened, just in time to see Grug walk off a cliff!

"Grug, we have to keep moving," Guy urged.

But Grug was on a roll. He came back to the tree, holding a huge, flat rock over his head.

"See, I got ideas. I got thoughts," he said. "Like this. I call it a mobile home. Isn't that something?"

But a huge bird flying overhead thought Grug's mobile home looked like a great landing pad.

Smoosh! The bird landed on the rock, smashing Grug into the ground.

But Grug jumped right up to show off his next

invention. He had taken a long, wooden board and propped it up on a rock, creating a kind of seesaw.

"I'm calling this one the 'lifterator,'" he said proudly.

Eep looked at her mother, worried. "Mom?"

Ugga nodded. "I know. It's bad."

Grug stood on the bottom of the lifterator, holding a huge boulder. He tossed the boulder onto the opposite end of his invention. The boulder crashed down, and Grug went flying up . . . and up . . . and up . . . until he was just a speck in the sky.

Zap! A bolt of lightning hit Grug, and he plummeted back to Earth.

"I almost feel sorry for him," Gran said.

Bam! Grug hit the ground hard.

"Ha! No, I don't," Gran cackled.

When Grug woke up, he found himself on a boat made from a giant turtle shell. All the Croods were in it, and Guy was steering. They were gliding across a glassy lake, and the base of the Mountain was on the other side.

Grug sat up, groaning, as Ugga tended to his bumps and bruises. She took off his wig.

"What are you trying to do, Grug?" she asked.

"I thought if I could have ideas like Guy, maybe Eep would listen to me," Grug said. "Maybe she wouldn't want to go to with Guy."

Ugga winced, realizing that Grug had overheard them talking in the tree the night before. "Oh, Grug, is that what this is all about?"

The shell boat glided onto the shore.

"We're here," announced Guy.

Suddenly the sky grew dark as thousands of birds flew overhead. Belt turned to Guy. "Da da daaa," he whispered ominously.

"No, we're close," Guy assured him. "We can make it."

The Croods were climbing out of the boat when *boom!* An explosion rocked the ground, and a plume of bubbling magma burst from the water on the other side of the lake.

"Know-it-all," Guy said to Belt.

Grug pointed to the base of the Mountain, where the mouth of a perfectly good cave waited for them. "Cave! Everyone inside. Hurry up! Let's go!"

But nobody moved.

"Come on!" Grug yelled.

"No," Eep said firmly.

Ugga was gentler. "No more caves, Grug," she said, stepping next to Eep.

Grug was stunned. "What?"

"We're gonna jump on the sun and ride it to Tomorrow with Guy," Gran said, joining her daughter and granddaughter.

"Wait, so you're all going to do this?" Grug asked.

His family was silent. Their answer was obvious.

Grug looked at Thunk, his son, his only son, the son who adored him.

"Thunk?"

"Sorry, Dad," Thunk said quietly, joining the others.

Grug felt like he had been punched by a monkey. Eep, he could understand. But Thunk? This was Guy's fault. Everything was Guy's fault. . . .

"You have to stop worrying for all of us," Eep said.

"It's my job to worry," Grug protested. "It's my job to follow the rules."

"The rules don't work out here," Eep countered.

Grug shook his head. "They kept us alive."

"That wasn't living," Eep said. "That was just . . . not dying. There's a difference."

Grug looked at his wife. Surely she would understand.

"Ugga—everyone—you have to listen to me," he pleaded.

The earth rumbled in the distance, and Ugga stood

her ground. Grug turned to face Guy, fury building inside him like a volcano about to explode. Then he heard Eep behind him.

"We'd be dead now if we'd listened to you," Eep said coldly, and Grug felt his heart tear out of his chest.

Eep didn't let up. "We have to follow Guy now."

"Guy?" Grug asked, raising an eyebrow.

"Guy, run," Ugga urged.

But it was too late. Grug lunged toward Guy, screaming. He tackled the boy, and they both went tumbling down an embankment.

CHAPTER 15

Guy jumped to his feet and ran as Grug chased him. The ground trembled under their feet.

"This is pointless," Guy called behind him. "We're running out of time. Everything is collapsing. You're being irrational and counterproductive."

"Big words anger me," Grug growled. "Keep talking!"

"Countermeasures," Guy shot back.

"That'll work!" Grug cried.

He backed Guy up into the side of a cliff. Belt threw everything he could find at Grug. The fruit squashed on his chest. The rocks just bounced off his head. Then Belt threw a clump of dirt right in Grug's eyes, blinding him.

"Remember how you were this morning?" Guy asked in a panic. "You changed, remember? Idea man? Modern man?"

Grug wiped the dirt from his eyes. He lifted up his massive arms, tightening his bulging muscles. His eyes blazed with all the intensity of his ancient ancestors.

"I . . . am . . . a . . . CAVEMAN!"

And then he lunged at Guy.

"No, no, no, wait!" Guy cried, but it was too late. They both fell over a waterfall . . . of tar. There was hardly a splash when they landed in the sticky black pool at the bottom. Slowly they began to sink. Belt quickly scampered on top of Guy's head.

"Aaargh, no!" Grug fumed. He couldn't move his arms! "What is this stuff that's saving you from my punches?"

"Tar," Guy replied, his voice hollow.

Grug recognized something in the tone of Guy's voice—utter defeat and despair. He stopped trying to punch Guy and tried walking to the shore. But he and Guy were stuck in the black goo up to their knees. The more he moved, the more he seemed to sink into the pit.

"Please, Grug. You have to stop struggling," Guy said.

"No! I have to get back to them!" Grug replied.

"Grug! Stop!" Guy yelled.

Guy's voice was serious, and Grug listened.

"No one gets out of this," Guy said softly. "Believe me."

Grug suddenly got it.

"Your . . . ?"

"Family. Yeah," Guy said, averting his eyes. The memory was still too painful to think about.

"Sorry," Grug said sincerely.

Guy took a deep breath. Maybe if Grug knew his story, he would understand. But it wasn't going to be easy to get the words out.

"I was little when it happened," Guy explained. "The last thing my parents told me was, 'Don't hide. Live. Risk. Follow the sun. You'll make it to Tomorrow.'"

A shaft of sunlight filtered through the dark clouds above, and Guy reached out and caught it with his palm. Grug finally understood.

"You followed the light," Grug said. "My daughter is a lot like you."

"No," Guy said. "She's like you. She loves you but always forgets to say it." He paused. "Just like you forget to tell her."

Grug had never considered this before. He'd assumed Eep didn't love him anymore because they were always arguing. But what if she thought the same about him? That would be terrible. He hated to admit it, but this Guy was pretty smart about things. And that was okay.

Grug looked right into Guy's eyes. "You're right," he admitted. "I guess I was just busy keeping them all alive."

"It's okay," Guy said. "That's what dads do."

Grug smiled. Guy was right again. And Grug had to get back to his family! "That's right, and we can't do that from here. Get us out!" he said to Guy.

Guy looked down at his pet. "Belt! Emergency Idea Generator, engage!"

Whack! Belt hit Guy on the head with a rock.

"Ow!" Guy wailed. But then his eyes lit up. "I've got it!"

Moments later the pair was ready to put Guy's plan into effect. They knew that Chunky the Macawnivore was searching for them in the trees nearby. This time, having him around would come in handy.

"Ta-daaaa!" Belt announced, as Guy and Grug held up the puppet he had made that looked like a female Macawnivore. The puppet's frame was made of bones, and it was covered with colorful feathers.

"Wow," Grug said, impressed.

"Yeah, I know," Guy said, but he didn't sound as enthusiastic. "He's doing the best with what he has. Let's go."

Belt jumped onto the shore and watched for the approaching Macawnivore as Grug and Guy got the puppet ready. Then Belt motioned with his paw. Chunky was on his way!

"There he is," Guy whispered. He nodded to Belt.

"Belt, I want romance, drama, sincerity. Move me."

Belt whipped out a flute and began to play. The Macawnivore stopped in his tracks and slowly padded toward the sound.

"Okay, he sees us!" Guy announced, excited.

Belt's tune became melodramatic.

Grug moved the bones he was holding, making the puppet's tail wiggle lamely back and forth.

"That's our cue. Now work it!" Guy urged him.

Grug worked the tail again, shaking it back and forth with as much feeling as he could muster.

Guy frowned. "He's not coming over. I don't think our puppet looks scared enough."

"Scared? I'll show you scared," Grug said. That was right up his alley. "Hand me those acting sticks!"

Guy gave him the bones attached to the puppet's head and front paws, and Grug went to work. He made the puppet shake violently with fear, and then added a wail of terror on top of it.

Suddenly Chunky leaped toward the Tar Pit, grabbing the puppet. He pulled it up out of the tar, bringing Grug and Guy along for the ride. They hung tightly on to the bones of the puppet frame.

"Okay, you're very good at this!" Guy told Grug. "Hold on!"

Chunky shook the puppet again, but this time it broke apart in Chunky's teeth. He turned and looked at Grug and Guy standing on the shore of the pit. He was angry.

"Du du duhhh," Belt sang ominously.

The Macawnivore lunged at Grug and Guy, and they started to run. Then they noticed that Chunky was slowly slipping backward. He was soon stuck in the tar!

Grug slapped Guy on the back. "Yes. You did it!"

When he tried to remove his hand, he realized it was stuck. At that moment, the rest of the Croods came running up.

"Grug!" Ugga cried.

"Dad!" Thunk added.

Grug was so happy to see his family. He began to wave . . . with Guy still stuck to his hand.

It looked bad, but Guy tried to assure the rest of the Croods that things were okay between the two of them.

The Croods didn't believe him at first, but there wasn't any time for Guy and Grug to explain. In the next moment, the ground underneath them began to tremble violently. Fiery meteors streaked across the sky.

"It's your call, Grug," Guy said.

Grug looked to the Mountain. It was time to finish what they had started.

CHAPTER 16

Guy led the Croods to the very top of the Mountain. As they neared the uppermost peak, they had to shield their eyes from the bright rays of the sun.

"Hurry! Come on! We're gonna make it!" Guy yelled.

Guy's Tomorrow was in their sights. There was a bridge of fluffy white clouds that seemed to lead right to the bright yellow sun. It looked solid, like they could walk right across it.

"You were right," Eep said, smiling at Guy.

"There it is," Guy said. "The sun. We can do it! We can ride it to Tomorrow."

Grug was amazed. It looked like Guy was right. Tomorrow was right there, so close that they could almost touch it.

But when they reached the top of the peak, hot

gases rising up from the split ground below burst the clouds. The fluffy white bridge disappeared, revealing the landscape for miles and miles in every direction. A green, grassy meadow stretched out on the other side of a deep ravine.

They all stared, confused. It was like Tomorrow had vanished from their eyes. There was no bridge to the sun.

Tremors began to shake the Mountain, rousing them from their stunned trance.

"Run!" Guy yelled.

But before they could get away, a large chunk of rock broke off underneath them. Grug pulled Eep and Guy away just in time, and all three rolled backward onto the dusty ground.

"I don't understand," said a bewildered Guy. "The sun was right here. It was right here."

KABOOM! The earth at the foot of the Mountain exploded, shooting a blanket of black ash into the sky. It was like night had suddenly fallen. Panicked, Ugga started to herd everyone back down the path that led to the base of the Mountain.

"We have to go back to that cave," she said. "Hurry, hurry, stay together. Let's keep moving. Everybody hold my hand."

Gran, Thunk, and even Guy and Eep hurried to follow her, too frightened to do anything else.

"Thunk, let's go!" Ugga ordered. "Everybody stay together."

Normally, Grug would have been leading the charge back to the cave. But not today. He peered into the curtain of black ash.

A wispy shaft of light struggled to reach him through the ash cloud. He held up his hand to feel it, and a beam of light settled on his palm.

He was enlightened.

He turned back to his family. They were huddled at the start of the path, waiting for him. Each and every one of them looked terrified. Normally, this would have made him happy. Scared meant safe.

But then was then. And this was . . . Tomorrow. Well, almost.

"Grug, what's wrong with you?" Ugga asked. "Grug, we'll die if we stay here!"

Grug didn't answer her. She approached him and talked to him softly. "Grug, listen to me. We have to get back to that cave."

Grug looked at his family. "No more dark. No more hiding. No more caves."

He paused. "What's the point of all this?" he asked,

motioning to the darkness and destruction all around them. "To follow the light."

Eep smiled. It was what she'd been feeling all along.

"I can't change," Grug told them. "I don't have ideas. But I have my strength. And right now that's all you need to get to Tomorrow."

Ugga shook her head. "No," she said. "We don't know what's over there. Maybe nothing. It's too risky."

"Life is risk. It's a chance," he said, believing it for the first time in his life.

Guy listened to Grug, entranced. Belt wiped a tear from his friend's eye.

"I'll take that chance," Guy said.

Grug picked up Guy and lifted him above his head.

"You know, I've wanted to throw you away ever since I met you," he said.

"Heh," Guy laughed meekly. "That's a joke, right?"

"What's a joke?" Grug asked, but he had a twinkle in his eye.

Belt quickly strapped on a helmet. This could go wrong in a thousand ways.

Grug hauled back with all his might, trying to remember what he had seen in the land below before the ash cloud came. He'd have to get Guy far over the ravine and safely onto the grassy field.

With a huge groan, Grug hurled Guy into the abyss. The Croods waited, silent, for some sign that he was okay. It seemed like an eternity had passed. Eep's lower lip began to tremble. And then . . .

Bwaaaaaaaaa!

The sound of a horn blared from the other side of the Mountain.

Ugga let out a breath. "He made it," she said. "He made it."

Grug turned to his son. "Okay, Thunk. Your turn."

Thunk looked up at his dad. He might not have a brain either, but he had figured out how this was going to go. "You're not coming, are you?"

"When you make it, so will I," Grug promised.

Thunk believed his dad. If anyone could find a way, it was Grug. He stood still as Grug hoisted him up and then hurled him off the Mountain.

Ugga walked up to Grug, holding Sandy in her arms. "You did good," she whispered in his ear.

Sandy looked up at her father. "Daddy."

Grug gently wiped a tear from Ugga's eye. Then he lifted her above his head and threw her.

On the other side of the Mountain, Thunk saw his mother come flying through the cloud of ash. He zig-zagged across the field like a football player and caught her in his arms before she hit the ground. Sandy giggled and clapped her hands.

Back on the Mountain, Grug turned to Gran next.

"No mush, just throw me," Gran said.

Grug lifted her above his head.

"Wait!" Gran called down, and Grug stopped. "You surprised me today. Lunkhead."

Grug smiled and tossed her off the Mountain. She landed safely on the other side.

"Still alive!" she cheered.

The Mountain trembled again, and more of the rock fell away around Grug and Eep.

"Time to go," Grug told his daughter.

Eep couldn't believe it. For days, all she had wanted to do was get as far away from her father as possible. And now she didn't want to leave him.

"No," Eep said desperately. "I have too much to say to you. I need to fix everything, and I don't have time."

"I can fix it," Grug said, and then he scooped her up in a tight embrace. Eep felt the love pouring out of her dad.

"This works good," Eep said. "What do you call it?"

"I was thinking of calling it a hug," Grug said. He cleared his throat, trying not to cry. "Because it rhymes with Grug. But you can change it if you want."

126

"No, I like hug," Eep said, and she hugged him back.

"I love you," Grug told her.

"Dad, I'm scared," Eep admitted.

And then her father said something she never thought she'd hear from him. "Never be afraid," he said, and he hoisted her up and hurled her into Tomorrow.

CHAPTER 17

Grug stumbled backward. He had used every ounce of strength to get Eep across the ever-widening expanse. Had she made it?

Then, miraculously, the ash cloud parted, and Grug saw his whole family safe on the other side. He waved to them one last time.

Grug had hurled everyone over the mountainside. But there was no one left to hurl Grug.

Another earthquake startled Grug, and now big, steaming rocks were falling from the sky. He spotted the entrance to a small cave and quickly ducked inside. There was nothing to do now but wait for the world to end around him.

To his surprise, Grug found that he didn't welcome the darkness of the cave. He picked up two of the stones that he had seen Guy use and struck them together. A spark ignited, and Grug quickly gathered some dried leaves and twigs together to make a flame.

"Hey, I did it," Grug said, proud of himself.

Another earthquake shook the cave, and Grug knew he didn't have much time left. But he could still leave his mark. He found a small puddle of mud in the cave and used it to paint a portrait of his family on the wall. There was Ugga, so beautiful, and Sandy, so adorable! There was Thunk, who looked just like him, and Eep, who acted just like him. He even painted Guy and Gran. And then he painted himself, protecting all of them in his big, strong arms, just like the old days.

Grug stood back to admire his work, looking longingly at the family he would never see again. Then the torch began to go out, and he leaned over to blow on it so he could look at the painting for as long as he had left.

When the flame flared up again, Grug was startled to see Chunky the Macawnivore in the mouth of the cave. The massive beast growled at him.

"Ah! Stay back! Stay back!" Grug yelled.

Chunky stopped growling and started blowing on the fading torch. He was just as frightened as Grug!

129

Realizing this, Grug reached out and stroked the now-gentle beast.

Soon Grug and Chunky were curled up together in the cave, watching the flickering light on the wall. Then Grug heard a familiar sound.

Bwaaaaa! Bwaaaa! It was Eep's shell! Grug rushed to the cave entrance and looked out. The world was falling apart around him. Hot magma bubbled up from the ground, rocks fell from the sky, and the earth was torn apart in a thousand places.

He heard the shell alarm sound two more times. His family was in trouble! Grug's heart started to race.

"They're in trouble," he told Chunky. Then he cupped his hands around his mouth and yelled out of the cave. "Hang on! I'm coming!"

Then his shoulders slumped as the scale of his problem sank in.

"How do I get across?" he wondered out loud. "Gotta think. What would Guy do? What would Guy do?" Chunky watched him curiously as he anxiously paced across the cave.

Then he stopped. He couldn't think like Guy. But he could think like Grug.

"What would *I* do?" he asked aloud.

He absently handed the torch to the Macawnivore.

"Hold this," he said, and then he closed his eyes, concentrating. A thought was beginning to form. "I . . . have . . . an . . . IDEA!"

This wasn't like the ride, or the shades, or the lifterator. This was a real idea. He knelt next to Chunky. He'd need the big cat's help once again.

Grug quickly sprang his plan into action. He located a giant rib cage of some long-dead animal on the mountaintop and covered it with sticky black tar. Then he found a nest of Piranhakeets in a nearby tree and jumped up, startling them. The birds immediately began to chase Grug.

Grug turned and ran toward Chunky.

"Run!" he yelled.

He leaped onto the Macawnivore's back and the beast obeyed, speeding up the Mountain. The ground began to break up all around them, but Chunky never lost his footing.

Chunky rushed into the giant rib cage, just as Grug had told him to. The Piranhakeets hit the cage in midflight and got their feet stuck to it, just as Grug had hoped. They flapped their wings, fighting to free themselves, lifting the cage off the ground in the process.

Grug took a giant tree branch and set it on fire. He held it behind the Piranhakeets, frightening them. They started to fly away from the fire—and toward the rift, which was exactly where Grug wanted to go.

As the Blimp-Cage flew above the fiery landscape, Grug noticed a pair of Trip Gerbils below. He jumped out of the cage and ran over to grab the gerbils. As he scooped them up, he noticed a scared Liyote hiding behind a rock. Grug swung the gerbils around his neck like a scarf and grabbed the Liyote.

He started to head back to the flying cage when he noticed Douglas, Thunk's pet Crocopup, looking forlornly around him. The poor beast still held Thunk's shell in his mouth. With a sigh, Grug jumped over a pool of steaming lava to rescue Douglas.

Then he heard a loud roar behind him, but Grug knew the sound wasn't coming from any animal. A massive current of heated gas and rock was speeding toward him. Once it hit him, it would all be over.

Grug caught up to the cage and tossed the rescued animals aboard. It just wasn't going fast enough to escape the cloud, so Grug pushed with all his might.

"Hold on," Grug instructed the creatures in the cage.

It worked! The Piranhakeets pulled the cage to the edge of the cliff seconds ahead of the massive gas cloud. Grug leaped off the cliff, trying to grab hold of the cage—but he couldn't reach. At the last second, Chunky stretched out his tail.

Grug grasped the tail just as the hot cloud hit them.

CHAPTER 18

On the other side of the Mountain, Eep blew her shell horn one more time. Sandy howled at her feet. Gran picked up Sandy to comfort her. A tear formed in Gran's eye. She was going to miss that lunkhead.

"We gotta go. It's not safe here," Guy said to Gran.

"I'll tell her," Gran replied.

But Eep continued to blow her horn. She looked at her grandmother and began to cry. Then, to her surprise, Gran started blowing on the horn.

"This is hard for all of us," Ugga began. "But Eep, if your dad were here, he would tell you to—"

"GET OUT OF THE WAY!"

"Wow, you sound just like him," Thunk said.

Ugga looked up in disbelief. Somehow, Grug was flying through the sky right toward them!

"GET OUT OF THE WAY!" Grug repeated. He wasn't sure he could steer the thing anymore.

"He did it!" Eep cheered.

Sandy clapped her hands. "Daddy!"

"He's riding the sun, but not very well," Guy realized. "Everybody out of the way!"

Grug crashed not too far from his family.

"Dad!" Thunk cried.

"Grug!" Ugga said happily.

Grug leaped out of the cage, ready for action. "Where's the danger? Who blew their shell?"

But he didn't see any danger. All he saw was his astonished family staring back at him.

Eep ran to him and hugged him ferociously, nearly knocking him down. "I love you, too," she told him.

The rest of the Croods ran to hug Grug, and he counted every one to make sure they were safe.

"One, two, three, four, five, six . . ." Then he put his arm around Guy. "And seven."

Belt squeaked and held up his paws, as if to say, *What about me?*

"And a half," Grug added.

The Trip Gerbils that Grug had rescued began to hug him, and Grug laughed.

"And eight, and nine . . ."

Douglas waddled up to Thunk and licked him.

"Douglas!" Thunk looked at his dad. "You saved him!"

"Well, a boy's got to have a pet," Grug said.

Then the Macawnivore rose up behind Grug, and everyone took a frightened step back.

"Turns out I'm a cat person," Grug said, grinning. He turned to pet Chunky and saw a tail sticking from his mouth. "Uh, no!" he scolded.

Chunky sheepishly opened his mouth, and the Liyote ran out.

The Croods gathered around, petting Chunky, but Eep walked to the edge of the new canyon.

"You really need to see this," she called to her family.

The ocean had flowed in to fill the new canyon. Peaceful green waves lapped against a bright, sandy shore. Grug stepped up beside Eep and grinned.

"We should go there," he said.

EPILOGUE

So the old world came to an end. But a new one began—
a new one filled with giant pets, suntans, and ocean
breezes.

My name is Eep, and if you haven't already guessed,
my family and I aren't exactly cavemen anymore. Our
world is still plenty harsh and hostile. But now we know
the Croods will make it.

Because we changed the rules. The ones that kept us
in the dark. And because of my dad, who taught us that
anyone can change. Well, sort of.

So from now on, we'll stay out here on the Beach . . .
where we can follow the light.